The DARK

DAYS of

HAMBURGER

HALPIN

The DARK

DAYS of

HAMBURGER

HALPIN

josh
berk

Alfred A. Knopf
NEW YORK

THIS IS A BORZOI BOOK PUBLISHED BY ALFRED A. KNOPF

Visit us on the Web! www.randomhouse.com/teens

Educators and librarians, for a variety of teaching tools, visit us at
www.randomhouse.com/teachers

Library of Congress Cataloging-in-Publication Data

Berk, Josh.
The dark days of Hamburger Halpin / by Josh Berk. — 1st ed.
p. cm.
Summary: When Will Halpin transfers from his all-deaf school into a mainstream Pennsylvania high school, he faces discrimination and bullying, but still manages to solve a mystery surrounding the death of a popular football player in his class.
ISBN 978-0-375-85699-0 (trade) — ISBN 978-0-375-95699-7 (lib. bdg.) —
ISBN 978-0-375-89551-7 (e-book)
[1. Deaf—Fiction. 2. People with disabilities—Fiction. 3. High schools—Fiction.
4. Schools—Fiction. 5. Bullies—Fiction. 6. Murder—Fiction. 7. Mystery and detective stories.]
I. Title.
PZ7.B442295Dar 2010
[Fic]—dc22
2009003118

The text of this book is set in 17-point New Baskerville.

Printed in the United States of America
February 2010
10 9 8 7 6 5 4 3 2 1

First Edition

To Jack and Rita Berk for filling my life with laughter,
love, and books, books, books . . .

PART One
The First Week

CHAPTER ONE

It is a cool September morning. The sun is breaking through the pines, and the air carries a tangy scent of freshness and renewal only to be found on the first day of school. I am rocking my plus-size Phillies sweatshirt and waiting with the others at the bus stop. Well, not exactly "with" them. As often happens when I'm out in the world, I place myself a little bit apart from the herd. I lean against a tree a few feet off to the side of a triangle formation of two cute girls and a dude. I get their names: A.J., Teresa, and Gabby. They hardly acknowledge me, so I return the favor. I have a lot on my mind anyway.

Will I survive at the mainstream school? Should I seduce Nurse Weaver to stay out of special ed? I don't have a proven talent for normal, and it strains the limits of credibility to come up with a scenario that involves seducing Nurse Weaver, the school district RN who did my hearing test. (I passed, barely, by guessing and promising to wear my hearing aids, which are already stashed in my pocket—sucker!) Still, it is a fun thought. Nurse Weaver is a cutie. Thinking about seducing her is certainly preferable to imagining doing sexual favors for the person who really holds my future in her hands: Superintendent Sylvia P. Zirkel.

I had to write a plea to SPZ to let me transfer from the deaf school to Carbon High. It was mostly lies, since I figured she wouldn't really understand the fight that forced my departure from the school for the deaf. Infights and deaf-world arguments rarely make sense to anyone else. She gave a distinctly wary OK, but I still have to be on her good side. If she deems it necessary, I will be bounced. Regardless, I will *not* allow myself to be taken advantage of by Superintendent Zirkel—a woman who looks like a skeleton in a Beatles wig and smells like beef. This is my solemn vow. Amen.

Nurse Weaver might have guessed that I was fumbling through the hearing test, but she was impressed with my lipreading skills. They are fantastic, if I do say so myself. I was one of the two best lip-readers at my old school (the other being my ex-"girlfriend," Ebony). I'll have to rely on lipreading to get by, since this school district is still relatively underfunded despite all the newly rich moving in on the fringes of coal country. CHS cannot afford a cool captioning system like some of the fancy schools over the river. There are no interpreters. There's no structured "inclusion" program. What they have is pretty much "sink or swim." And from what I hear (so to sign, *not* speak), sink is the more common outcome.

The school bus comes, and I cruise on. Geez. I didn't factor in this being so terrifying, seeing these unfamiliar faces all scrubbed and happy. Who *are* these people? There is one guy, a half-asleep-looking weirdo slouching in the back, who seems like he should be on a prison bus. I plop down on the first seat behind the bus driver.

The bus driver is a wiry and dangerous-looking man with a bizarre beard that rings his tanned face like an upside-down halo. Even though it is pretty cold out, he is wearing sandals, which reveal unnervingly long toenails. He is also eating a family-size bag of pork rinds for breakfast.

A cocky kid who gets on at a stop after mine says something to Jimmy Porkrinds about his sandals, to which he replies, "My feet, my business." Pretty deep. Someone should engrave it on a plaque and/or make it into an inspirational poster to hang in bathrooms. For the rest of the trip, J.P. talks to himself. I *love* people who talk to themselves. Through the rearview mirror, I lip-read some strange stuff coming out of his mouth. Stuff that might have been song lyrics: "Dig, dig, dig the hole, hidey-hidey hole" and "Joke the mole, smoke a bowl." I write in my notebook: JIMMY PORKRINDS = ADDLED POTHEAD OR GIFTED LYRICIST?

I also watch a few conversations from the rows behind me. Several kids, including Teresa and Gabby, have brought large envelopes with them and are waving them around. Those without envelopes seem a little sad. Somebody grabs Gabby's envelope, and a shiny piece of paper falls out and flutters to the ground. She freaks out and dives to catch it as if it was a baby falling to its death. "Dude, I am not missing that party," she says. "No way." She grabs it back up and carefully slides it into the envelope again with a smug expression. A.J. looks like he's not sure if he should laugh or cry. Join the club. Before long, with a fabulous mutter of "Watch yo' ass, Philip Glass" from J.P., we have arrived at school.

CHAPTER TWO

My day begins with a meeting in the principal's office. Principal's office already? Am I in trouble on the first day? I admonish myself. You are quite the miscreant, William Badboy Halpin.

Have to be careful not to look like some weirdo laughing to myself here. I do feel a bit nervous walking in that door labeled PRINCIPAL KROENER. Even at the deaf school, we heard about Kroener. He supposedly threw a kid through a window for chewing gum. I was hoping I could get all the way to graduation without ever having to meet him. I've forgotten to put my hearing aids back on, but he doesn't notice. I can hear a little with them, but I hate them. I know I still don't hear what everyone else does, they give me intense headaches, and I hate being stared at like I have six heads. When I put them on, all eyes go straight to my ears. No one notices my dashing movie star looks or bodybuilder's physique. Understandably.

Kroener is on a phone call and distractedly welcomes me into his office. He gestures for me to take a seat and scatters some papers as he does. I spy with my little eye a particular sheet of paper labeled "Will Halpin Individual Education Program." The fact that I require an IEP reminds me that I'm still on the banks of the mainstream. And though the sheet is upside-down from where I sit, I can make out the basics. Apparently, I'm "profoundly deaf yet intellectually capable." This *yet* pisses me off! It's the kind of thing some of my old classmates would have formed a protest committee over. I'm usually the type to let things slide, which maybe was why I was somewhat of an outsider even among my own peeps.

I see too that I have high marks for my ability to lip-read, and it's also noted that I'm excellent at sign language. A kiss of the hand to you. My ability to speak is listed as "adequate," which makes me smile inside, since I barely said a word to Nurse Weaver. I hardly speak at all, and I really don't like talking to people I don't know well. People have laughed at the way I talk, and I don't altogether know what the hell I'm saying. I've had a million arguments about how I should probably just get over this and be proud of my deafness, but I remain unconvinced. That kind of thinking is part of the reason I left my old school.

Kroener slams down the phone and gives me my schedule. He seems like he is actually trying to be nice. He has learned a few signs and stumbles through "Welcome to our school." He hands me a letter that basically says the same thing and a map, which I hope I will be able to figure out. "Consider me welcomed," I sign, throwing Kroener a big, only partly insincere, grin. Tall and wide, with a head shaped like a bullet, Principal Kroener tries to smile back, but it looks like it doesn't fit his face. I wave awkwardly and skedaddle.

First up, first class. I'm good with maps, probably from constantly playing video games (take that, video game critics!), so I easily find the room for American history. I'm stepping in, feeling like an astronaut on alien soil as my foot lands on the other side of the threshold. There is no time to contemplate this giant leap for Halpin-kind, however, because I am immediately overwhelmed. And it seems I'm not the only one.

The teacher, a pear-shaped, balding man whose ID badge identifies him as Mr. Arterberry, appears to be even more unsure of what to do with me. Nurse Weaver assured me that she had filled the teachers in, so they know all about my "primary mode of understanding" being lipreading and that I am "strong textually," which I assume means that I read and write well. She's right—I enjoy words. They are like music to my ears.

Mr. A. has a seat for me off in a corner of the room. This will allow me to read lips of teacher as well as students and thus benefit from the fantastic scholarly wisdom offered by both lecture and class discussion. But it also makes me feel shoved aside, sort of like a houseplant. Will someone at least remember to prune and water me?

The first thing I notice is this: public school girls are freaking *hot. Nice.* I try to focus on that and not on the sinking feeling that it might be way harder not to fail here than I thought. It's only been a few seconds since class started, and Arterberry apparently has already forgotten Nurse Weaver's instructions. Even though I have always been exceptionally good at lipreading (blue ribbon at Camp Arrowhead!), I need to actually see the lips. Even in the best situations, I'm likely to miss a few words in the middle of a sentence. Arterberry keeps turning around or covering his mouth with his flabby arm while writing on the board. Plus, although I realize that the Americans with Disabilities Act can't force him to get rid of his bushy lip beast, a basic sense of fashion and/or hygiene should compel him to at least trim his 'stache.

The class ends before I have any idea what era of history we were even talking about. The American Revolution or maybe the Teapot Dome scandal? At the deaf school, every teacher knows sign language, and they have these captioning systems so everything shows up as text on a screen in addition to the lecture. Have I made a terrible mistake coming here? But I got so tired of the squabbles. Are you deaf enough? Strong deaf? Weak deaf? I just wanted to hang out and relax—not have to prove so much. I simply don't have a problem with hearing people. I always ended up defending them. Which landed me here. And now I'm not so sure. . . .

Ah, but the girls.

One specimen, a perky little type, answers so many questions that it is easy to figure out her name even through Arterberry's swath of mustache hair. "Yes, Mindy?" "Miss Spark?" "Right you are, Mindy." "Mindy, Mindy, Mindy." Deaf people are also good at reading emotion as well as content, and it is easy for me to see that Mindy Spark is already Mr. Arterberry's least favorite student.

And then there is a girl I'm pretty sure is named Leigha. Mindy says her name a few times ("Right, Leigha?" "How 'bout it, Leigha?" "Oh my God, remember this one time, Leigha?"), so I get it. This Leigha is an unqualified beauty. Her eyes shine like steel, and her perfect face is the face in a dream you never even knew you were capable of having. Perfect. I write it down in my little notebook. MOST BEAUTIFUL GIRL IN THE WORLD = LEIGHA-MIA. PERKY CHICK = MINDY SPARK PLUG. Then I write an observation about a weirdo from the bus. I don't know his name yet. Unlike Mindy, he answers no questions and spends the whole class staring at his fingers. SCUZZY GUY LOVES HIS FINGERS.

I hope this stuff will be on the test.

CHAPTER THREE

Math class follows Arterberry's fabulous romp through . . . the War of 1812? The Industrial Revolution? Who the hell knows? Like Arterberry, the math teacher gives me a seat off in the corner. I am actually glad to be out of the way, because what looks like impromptu hijinks have broken out in the middle of the room. A bigger dude spikes some dork's math book into another corner.

I decide to amuse myself by stealing a glance at the seating chart so I can learn some more of my classmates' names—just the sort of sneaky deaf detection I'm aces at. My desk is close enough to the teacher's that I can see part of it. A few things become clear regarding my classmates, and I make copious notes.

The beautiful girl from history is Leigha Pennington, an

appropriately lovely name. The scary guy who loves his fingers is Chuck Escapone. Dwight Carlson is a sort of clueless-looking nerd. One of the large football guys is named Travis Bickerstokes. A name that belongs to an empty seat reads "Pat Chambers." Where have I heard of him? And then I spot a name that has to be a typo: Purple Phimmul.

Can a person's name really be Purple? I look up. The person, a girl, who presumably really is named for a crayon, sits right next to Leigha. The two seem to be friends, even though Purple is hardly one of the pretty girls. She does seem rich, though, with what look like pricey clothes and pricier jewelry. Purple is round, and her lump of a head is framed by hair that has the frizzy and stringy appearance of a scarecrow caught in a windstorm. She, in fact, sort of looks like a female me.

The math teacher, who has just written her name on the board and dotted the *i* with a heart, is named Miss Prefontaine. Prefontaine eventually stops the book tossers, and when class begins, I am happy to see that she is very good at speaking clearly; I can see her lips and read every word. However, I feel like I should get my eyes checked when the *content* of her words registers. She is blatantly flirting with some of the football player guys in the back of the class. Like, *really* blatantly.

"Now, boys," Miss Prefontaine says, taking the pen she had been sucking on out of her pinkly lipsticked mouth, "settle yourselves down."

"Why don't you come over here and help settle me?" says a football guy, walking in late. It's Pat Chambers, the quarterback.

Of course. That's where I know that name. Football is huge around here, and his exploits throwing a ball make the news all over Pennsylvania.

Pat tosses wink after wink at Miss Prefontaine like she's his personal wide receiver. Leigha Pennington looks like she's going to gag. This makes me strangely happy.

Miss Prefontaine is young for a teacher but definitely much older than the high school student she apparently wishes she still was. She wears questionable makeup and way too much perfume. I have a good sense of smell and am sure that Prefontaine wears the exact same perfume as Leigha—a burnt roses scent. (What? So I happened to sniff Leigha's hair in the hallway.)

I get the distinct feeling that Prefontaine used to be ugly and went on one of those TV makeover shows or got a face transplant or something. She seems to be trying to use her newly minted hotness to live a better version of her passed youth. I mean, she couldn't have been cool in high school if she loved math, right? But now she has power. And a huge amount of cleavage. Which might be the same thing. Ah, such luscious power . . .

I add to my notebook: MISS PRE-FAB-VAIN = FORMER NERD? and MISS PREFONTAINE'S KNOOBS = FORMER A CUPS?

She is wearing a low-cut silky shirt unbuttoned to its plunging depths. When she bends over, I catch a glimpse of her tattoo: a dolphin leaping out from the left cup of her lacy black bra. *Distracting.* I look over at the paper of the guy next to me to try to catch an equation I missed. His whole page is filled with drawings of tiny leaping marine mammals.

"I would come over there and settle you down," Prefontaine says to Pat, flicking her tongue against her top teeth, "but you'd like that too much."

The dolphin drawer sees me looking at his paper. He whispers something to me. I point to my ears and make a head-shaking face.

"Y-O-U M-U-S-T B-E T-H-E N-E-W D-E-A-F K-I-D," he signs. Well, how about that? It isn't real sign language, just the one-letter-at-a-time version that hearing people (usually girls) learn sometimes. We call it finger spelling. He continues, pointing to himself: "D-E-V-O-N."

I finger-spell back: "W-I-L-L."

We talk back and forth like this for a little while, me giving everybody a chance like good old Mom had suggested. His last name is Smiley, which makes me laugh. Then he asks for and receives my screen name so we can chat online sometime.

"C-A-N Y-O-U B-E-L-I-E-V-E T-H-E-M?" he asks me, pointing a thumb toward Pat and Prefontaine. I shake my head.

And then Miss Prefontaine catches Devon and me signing to one another. She says something to the class that I don't see. Maybe: "Well, well, well, it seems our hefty deaf newcomer and Mr. Smiley are an item." Hopefully *not*.

Now there's a disturbing soundless chorus of shaking faces. A girl named Marie is scribbling something down. What is she, a reporter? Is the alleged romance between me and Devon Smiley going to be front-page news in the *Coaler Chronicle*? Beautiful Leigha is laughing. At me. Pat Chambers and his football friends are punching and slapping each other happily.

Pat actually laughs so hard that he literally falls off his chair in his unbridled glee. Damn.

I make another addition to my notebook: STAY AWAY FROM SMILEY GUY. If he is at the bottom of the food chain, so low that even teachers and C-listers rip on him, Devon is someone I can't *afford* to be seen with. I spend the rest of the class with my head down learning very little math. Finally, the bell rings (sound-impaired discriminators!). Time for lunch.

CHAPTER FOUR

I sort of want to skip lunch and find somewhere to be alone and clear my head, but I am freaking hungry. It has been, after all, about two hours since I last ate. And, besides, who among us can pass up the culinary delights offered in a high school cafetorium? This is a strong draw despite the well-documented and universally known social horrors of high school lunch. Who do I sit next to? What if I can't find a seat? What if I spill Sloppy Joes on my special first-day outfit?

My plan B is to smuggle my food into the bathroom, hole up in a stall, and eat atop the toilet like a smack-shooting junkie. Crap. It seems this will be thwarted by a large, shiny-headed bald man patrolling the perimeter of the cafetorium. Name badge check: Mr. Yankowski, a teacher. Yanky-Wanky seems to take his duty as lunch proctor as a sacred sojourn, prowling around like an attack dog aching to pounce. This goes in my notebook: YANKOWSKI = YANKY-WANKY = LORD SHINY-HEAD OF THE CAF.

I really feel like I just need a minute to collect myself, but it's too crowded to hide out solo in a corner. God, where do I go? I know there isn't going to be a big table filled with cool deaf people to sit with. I'm not that dumb. Or am I? What am I doing here?

I plop down at the edge of a table with a few open seats and look around furtively. Bodies turn from me as if we are oppositely charged magnets. Chairs scoot. Eyes avert. Chatty people are everywhere. It can be really overwhelming for a lip-reader to be in such a hivelike atmosphere. See, I can't turn off my ability to read lips, so it is like "hearing" a thousand conversations at once. A million voices, snippets, and fragments overlapping—getting lost, then standing out, then getting lost again. Someone says, "Wasn't that test terrible?" But I can't see/hear the response of the person she's talking to, so I read as response the non sequitur from the guy next to her: "Tim's the balls on drums!"

It's like watching TV while someone else works the remote. No, better yet: imagine yourself sitting in a room with a hundred TVs turned up loud while you whirl around on a Sit & Spin at a dizzying speed, trying to follow the plot. The only way to not totally lose my head is to intently focus on one person and—here's the trick—not get caught. Most folks aren't too keen on having a big deaf fatty eyeballing them. I'd love to be wrong about this, but it is unlikely.

I scan the room for someone interesting. Immediately in

front of me is my classmate from math, Dwight Carlson. It is sort of fun watching him try to figure out how to open the milk carton. Is he really that stymied? Noted: DWIGHT CARLSON = OUTWITTED BY BEVERAGE CONTAINERS. Chuck Escapone is also visible, but do I want to know what that guy has to say? What goes on in that mind? Look around . . . look around. OK, Purple Phimmul it is. Congratulations, Ms. Rich But Not So Pretty.

My target jams a pair of enormous gold sunglasses onto her face—a dangerous turn of events because now I can't tell if she sees me staring at her. Still, I press on. I have so many questions. Why is she named Purple? Is there a whole rainbow of Phimmuls at home? Is there an Uncle Aqua? An Aunt Chartreuse?

Purp is talking on her cell, eating candy bars, and ignoring her Fawning Public. FP will have to make do with whatever crumbs of attention she gives them while she gabs with a mysterious stranger on the other line. I suspect it is her father.

"Daddy," she whines (a telling clue, no?), "my balance is low again."

Daddy's response appears to be less than satisfactory.

"But I need a new dress for the party. I need to go shopping!" she yips. "Shopping, dammit!" She is yelling this consumerist battle cry, this war whoop of the mall. "Shopping, dammit! Shopping, dammit! Shopping, dammit!" She then snaps the phone shut like a queen snapping her fingers at a servant.

She glares at one of her minions as if it's *her* fault the Phimmul account is low. The minion lowers her eyes and scrambles to appease her. How does Purple do this? How does she get these people wrapped around her pudgy finger? And is the dress possibly for that party the people on the bus were talking about? What *is* this party that has my non-peers so wound up?? For a second I feel one of Purp's friends staring at me, so I look quickly away.

But, still, I'm thinking: What is your secret, Purple Phimmul? What is your secret?

CHAPTER FIVE

Gym is bad for any fat kid just on principle. When I found
out that at CHS I would have to swim (and that, no, there really
was no way out of it), I considered getting one of those old-
timey bathing suits with shoulder straps in order to provide
adequate man-boob coverage. Maybe I'd grow a handlebar
mustache too and pretend it was part of a 1900s revival look I
was going for. But it turns out that they don't sell 1900s-style
bathing suits at Wal-Mart, and I couldn't get my mom to order
me one on eBay. Perhaps, I think, I should go to the other extreme and don a Speedo. Might it be awesome to see my classmates' expressions as I strut out sporting a banana hammock?
But I only have the gut, not the guts. So I just wear a regular
pair of green swimming trunks, which offer neither fat con-
cealment nor risk-taking pride. As I emerge from the stall, I notice a few pointings and laughings. One or two guys try to slap

me on the love handles. Being fat might not be that great of a thing to be, but it sure seems to bring joy to certain others. Glad to oblige. Turd bags.

Devon Smiley is skinny but in a droopy sort of way. He seems to have no muscles. Pat and his jock buddies, including a rodent-looking football guy whose jersey identifies him as D. JONKER, apparently find his body hilarious. After I finish accepting my hazing, I slink into the corner, fashion my Phillies beach towel into a sarong, and watch the two of them screw with Devon. I'm guessing at the exact wording here, but the spirit of the conversation is clear.

"Hey, Dev," Pat says, approaching Devon with a look of mock seriousness on his face. "You been working out?"

Devon narrows his eyebrows like he is looking down a microscope at a confusing specimen. "How's that?" he says.

"He said," declares D. JONKER, "that you're looking diesel (*something something*)."

I slide around to the other side of the room and focus hard so I can continue to see this fascinating exchange.

"Hey, are you using the juice?" D. JONKER asks.

"Come again?" Devon says.

"How exactly do you get pecs like that?" Pat says, poking Devon's pale and sunken chest. "Me and Derrick are dying to know your secret."

I make a mental note. The *D* in D. JONKER is for Derrick. I had been thinking Dick.

"I think he's (*something something*) steroids," D. JONKER says.

"Only one way to find out!" they yell in unison, pouncing on Devon like a murder of crows on a field mouse.

After one impressively smooth movement (what, do they practice this stuff?), Pat and D. JONKER are holding Devon's shorts like a championship trophy while Devon, nude except for flip-flops, scrambles back into the stall.

"Yep," D. JONKER says, although I'm sure he didn't actually see anything. "You don't get balls that tiny unless you're juicing. Are those your nads, Smiley, or are you smuggling peas?"

Devon's retreating form makes me think of office supplies: two scrawny pencils jammed into eraser-pink trapezoids of butt.

Mr. Fatzinger (who introduced himself to me earlier, inspiring an addition to my notebook: GYM CLASS COACH = FATZY McFATPANTS) hears the commotion and sticks his head into the locker room and yells something like "Knock it the hell off and get out here for class or I'll (*something something*) Principal Kroener."

Apparently, this threat holds more water than the pool because everyone shuts up quickly. We all begin filing out, as orderly as soldiers, except for Devon, who is still hiding au naturel in the stall. Pat has Devon's shorts behind his back. He then passes the shorts to D. JONKER, who pretends to dribble them. He jukes left, jukes right, and throws them into the toilet. And then he flushes. Score: Usual Jock Jerks 1, Usual Hapless Victims 0.

CHAPTER SIX

When the day is finally over, I find my bus and crash into the first seat like a wrecking ball. I am shell-shocked and stunned, rattled by the enormity of it all, wondering what the fudge I have gotten myself into. I thought it'd be easier to enter this world, but I am now even more of a watcher, spying on my own life.

No one has exactly walked up and introduced themselves. Still, my notebook is slowly filling with names and critical information. Thanks to peeking at seating charts, checking out football jerseys, some lipreading, and the weird trend of girls wearing jewelry with their names spelled out in big gold script, I have started to piece together my class roster.

On the bus ride home, those big rearview mirrors installed so the driver can (in theory) keep an eye on the throng make espionage easy. I watch my fellow passengers' faces, read their lips, enter their conversations from afar while they unwittingly spill their secrets. They say more about themselves than they mean to, more than they even know. The way one kid leans over the seat in front of him, laughing along with someone else's joke—it shows how desperately he wants to fit in. The way one guy ignores a girl behind him but puts his arm up on the seat inches from hers shows his true feelings. And the fat deaf kid in the front, craning his neck and staring? He's a pretender. By putting so much effort into paying attention to others, is he trying not to think about himself? Will one more slight make him crumble into a pile of dust? What does he want? Who is he hoping he really is? Let's table these . . . for later.

So what's happening on this bus? The most interesting stuff is in the back. All the cool kids sit in the back. It is pretty much a directly rising slope of coolness from the front of the bus to the back. From me to a weird skinny guy in a football shirt who clearly isn't on the team to Marie (whose last name is Stepcoat) to the trio from my morning bus stop: A. J. Fischels, Teresa Lockhart, and Gabby Myers. If you keep going, you'd fly out the back of the bus onto the road itself and land in the cars belonging to the kids far too cool to ever set foot on a bus. I wish I had a damn car, or even a license. I sketch out this equation in my notebook. It all makes sense, but then I look out the window and clearly see Devon Smiley drive by in his car. He has a car? Devon Smiley may be an exception to all the rules that normally apply to humanity. Let's keep an eye on that one.

I watch the football fan talk to no one about the upcoming game and then turn around. A.J., Teresa, and Gabby are too far back for me to see in the mirror. I have to subtly turn around in my seat to see what nuggets they are offering. A.J.'s expression is dark, his body language a hunched ball of fury. The change from his cheery baby face is quite startling. Without drawing attention to myself, I smoothly rotate in my seat and watch.

"Don't be sad," Gabby is saying, messing his hair like a grandmother soothing a toddler. "I still think you're cool."

"Gabby," A.J. says, "I believe it should be (*something*) clear by now that no one cares what you think. About anything."

"Ow," says Teresa. "Burn." She then jumps into the seat in front of them and spins around, so I miss the rest of whatever she has to say.

What A.J. has to say is roughly: "He's just, he's just such a (*something something something*), you know? I never wanted to go to his stupid party anyway."

"Yeah, right," says Gabby, laughing. "You're telling me that if he gave you a playing card, you wouldn't accept it?"

"If he gave me a playing card, I'd throw it back in his . . . uh, playing face" is A.J.'s witty retort. At least I think that's what he said. "Playing face"?

Gabby laughs again. Then Teresa seems to say something, probably laughing too, or so it seems from the way her ball of curly auburn hair shakes. Suddenly A.J. sees me looking at them.

I try to quickly look out the window, acting interested in a billboard for a rock band on tour. Before I can pull it off, though, there is an instant where our eyes meet and lock hard.

"What?" A.J. shouts. (Yes, I can tell, even without benefit of volume, when someone's shouting.) "What the hell are you looking at?"

He bares his teeth, and foam forms on his lip like a rabid dog. He then gives me the universal sign everybody knows: two upraised middle fingers.

In my head I call this the GAJBF, for Great A.J. Bus Fiasco. (Did I mention that I like acronyms? Yeah.) A hot flush of embarrassment spreads up my neck and stays there. I keep my eyes down, peering into nothing more interesting than the gouges pocking the green pleather in front of me.

The mortifying diamond of the DEAF CHILD AREA announces to one and all that my stop is next. This stupid sign haunts my life. As the bus lurches to a halt, I get up, lumber swiftly down the three steps, and head toward home. But I can't help myself and cast one last glance back. A. J. Fischels's head is down, his shoulders slumped. He appears to be writing something in a secret notebook of his own. I would *love* to see that. Who made A.J. so livid? Who's throwing this big-deal party? And what does he mean by a playing card? Also, what did Mom make for dinner? Hope it's lasagna.

CHAPTER SEVEN

Next day at school. History class. Farterberry has made a disturbing announcement. Our class, it seems, will soon be taking a trip to something called Happy Memory Coal Mine. Ever-perky Mindy Spark shoots up her hand to say something like "Oh my God! I've been there (*something something*) Girl Scouts! Remember, Leigha? They do this (*something something*) they shut off all the lights and it's totally black!" As she speaks, she whips her head around with such excitement that her blond ponytail flops like a dying fish. Leigha Pennington nods ever so slightly in reserved agreement. Oh, Leigha.

The rest of the class, except for me and Chuck Escapone, seems to share Mindy's boundless enthusiasm. I'm not afraid of the dark, but when you rely on the sense of sight to speak and hear, being in total darkness with a bunch of mostly strangers is just creepy. Chuck, I am noticing, never responds to anything.

His eyelids did, I think, open slightly more than their usual half-shut stupor. Perhaps to Chuck Escapone this is the equivalent of jumping up and dancing with Mindy-like glee.

Escapone excluded, my classmates' faces light up, and they all start talking at once, which sucks. While I can't tell what anyone is specifically saying, I get the basic premise. Most are psyched beyond belief, while I am filled with dread beyond, uh . . . something dreadful. Only a few minutes into the new day and my stomach is lurching and my throat is closing in on itself.

"Now, class!" Arterberry says, actually standing where I can see him and enunciating under his big mustache. "Control yourselves, please!" But the class does not control themselves. Can you believe it? Even though he said "please," they *still* do not settle down. Shocking!

He writes "THE COAL-MINING EXPERIENCE" on the board for the benefit of the few paying attention. "Tonight's assignment: pages 114 to 133 in your text." I look around the room to see how this assignment will be received. Some students copy it down dutifully; others make no pretense that they are going to do the work. D. JONKER is one of those who write it down. Pat looks over at him like his buddy suddenly smells terrible. He doesn't say a word, but it is obvious what he means. "You're not seriously going to do this lame assignment, are you?" But D. JONKER apparently *is* going to do it. Maybe he comes from a coal-mining family like me? Maybe our ancestors all worked together in the mines. Maybe they were friends? Maybe someday we'll be . . . Yeah.

A lot of people have recently moved to our humble corner

of the world from New York (where, apparently, there are no more unfilled apartments). Do any of them care that the little kids who spent fourteen hours a day in the mines could have been their classmates' grandparents? Do they even get that? I mean, they must have noticed that our football team is called the Coalers, right?

A few more people appear to be a little interested when Arterberry says, with a twinkle in his eye, "This is an especially interesting passage in your text because there's a ghost story. . . ."

Now, I have always loved ghost stories. Perhaps because people often seem to vaguely sense my own presence while rarely acknowledging it. I've been brushed off like a specter, a chill. . . .

The sound-discriminatory bell announces the end of history class. Would it kill them to get a strobe light to flash when class ended? Or maybe a beautiful girl who could hold up a sign for me like in boxing matches? I pick up my books and begin my journey to math class. What wonders will The Dolphin have for us today?

CHAPTER EIGHT

When I slink in, Miss Prefontaine has already started her
"lesson." I scamper to my houseplant-seat. Devon Smiley is at
the extreme front and far end of the row, making him my clos-
est human contact. It is just a fluke of the seating chart, no
more meaningful than the fact that Dwight Carlson sits right
next to Pat Chambers, but Devon apparently takes it as cosmic
proof we are meant to be best buds. I do not feel precisely the
same way. Devon has a dumb ponytail. He smells faintly of
nacho cheese. He uses a monogrammed handkerchief to wipe
his nose. By insisting on being my friend, he is seriously threatening my incredibly cool status at CHS. (Kidding, of course,
but still . . .)

Prefontaine is so absorbed in making flirty faces while
"teaching" that she forgets to keep her mouth where I can see
it. We are supposed to figure out the distance an object will fall

if the angle is forty degrees and the height is forty feet (*something something*) and the rate of a falling body (*something something*). Lipreading is exhausting in the best of circumstances, and these are definitely not those circumstances. I try to spy off of Devon's paper, which makes him really happy. He writes a note to me on the corner of the page. "Hello, William!" I hate when people call me William and really don't want to get caught passing notes with Devon.

I sneak my history textbook out of my bag, hoping to pick up where I left off reading about mining. I start flipping through this chapter:

> The year was 1901. Coal miners lived a dangerous life, working long hours many feet below the earth's surface. Accidents were an inescapable part of a miner's world. Floods, explosions, and cave-ins were always possibilities.

I have to say, I get into it. Then something flitters in my peripheral vision. I ignore it. It won't go away. I hate that. Then it is close—right in front of my face, in fact—too close to ignore. A hand. I know what it signifies before I lift my gaze. Prefontaine is waving, doing that obnoxious gesture that means "Hello! I'm freaking talking here!" I try to pretend that I am actually paying attention, but I am nabbed. My face flushes the hot red of an embarrassed fatty. Of course she would ignore me 99 percent of the time but turn and stare at me just

the moment that I'm, of all things, doing homework for another class. Couldn't it at least have been porn?

And then she zings me a second time! Again, I have no idea
what she says. I just see Miss Prefontaine turn her back on me,
and then I watch the class crack up. Was it "Well, well, well, Mr.
Big Deaf Fatty thinks he's too good for us?" Or "Mr. Halpin
would rather look at pictures of coal miners than me? What
does that say about him, class? Do the math!"

I try not to look anywhere. My eyes fall on Devon. Without
looking at me, he makes these letter shapes with his left hand.
"W-H-A-T A B-U-N-C-H O-F A-S-S-H-O—" And then he points to the
clock. Saved by the bell. And by Devon Smiley, at least a bit.
Hmm . . .

CHAPTER NINE

Time for the joyride that is the bus trip home. Retards sit in the front, so there I am. Simple deduction. (I can hear the voices of Mom, a bevy of guidance counselors, and the entire self-esteem industry revving up for a speech, but please, folks, hold your breath. For once, shut up. It's just a joke. If I can take it, so can you.)

I watch the crowd, anxious to see if I can get more information about yesterday's card drama. At first I see the weird football fan raving. "We are going to kill Wilkes, how 'bout it!" he says. This guy has the coordination of a drunk walrus combined with the physique of a nine-year-old girl. Why does he say "we" when he is not on the team? I notice that his book bag has his name written on it with marker. I put it into my notebook: PLANDERS = INSECURE JOCK FAWNER.

"Yeah!" Planders yells, punching the back of the seat in front of him. "We're gonna kill 'em! Undefeated in the new stadium." Then he says something that baffles me for a minute until I realize he is throwing a bit of Spanish in there. I'm pretty sure he said, "Thank you, *número* 45!"

Marie Stepcoat, the girl from math, who's wearing one of those name necklaces, rolls her eyes at this burst of school spirit, like she is way above all that, even though I am pretty sure she is not. I guess we all enjoy having someone to make us feel better about ourselves. Look at me, ripping on Planders's physique. This from a guy with the body of a sedentary manatee. Before long, Jimmy Porkrinds lurches the bus toward my stop, and day two is over.

I storm into my house and head straight for the kitchen. I am ready for an after-school snack that could easily be mistaken for a second lunch. For ten. Slices of cheese eaten right out of the wrapper, two pickles, a bowl of ice cream. I suck it all down like a stoner on a binge. It doesn't make me feel better. Just fatter. My pants (which are already my designated "fat pants") are tight, and I feel gross about the whole thing. But I eat one last giant scoop of ice cream anyway. Damn.

I bust out *Freedom Isn't Free: The Story of America,* and I flip it open to the assigned chapter and quickly find where I had left off. What had started as mild interest suddenly turns to a lump of anthracite in my throat. Right there in black and white is mention of a coal miner who not only was deaf but also, apparently, is me.

> Cave-ins were not unusual and death lurked around every corner. Even in this cruel history, some events stand out as

unusually tragic. Take, for example, the case of William Halpin. "Dummy" Halpin, as he was known, was a deaf coal miner who worked in the mines of northeastern Pennsylvania. Halpin was able to mine quite well, reports say, despite being unable to communicate normally with the other miners.

July 9, 1901, began as a typical day for Dummy and his crew. Dummy took the lead position, driving deeper into the shaft.

William Halpin? A deaf person with my name had been living right here in northeastern Pennsylvania? Too weird. I stop and imagine how Pat and his crew will be cracking up at the phrase "driving deeper into the shaft." It *is* sort of funny. The text continues:

Halpin's fellow miners heard a loud splintering from above, a sign they recognized as the foreshadowing of a possible collapse. They purportedly screamed, "Dummy," but to no avail. Sadly, he could not hear them and was out of reach, making a rescue impossible. While the other miners scrambled to safety seconds before the mine collapsed, Halpin was crushed to death.

For weeks following the collapse, townspeople and other miners reported seeing or hearing the ghost of Dummy

Halpin near the spot of the cave-in, scratching at the ground, clawing to get out from under the rubble.

I stare at the words on the page. It is as if a unicorn has entered my room. Is Will "Dummy" Halpin a relative? My great-grandfather? Why hadn't I heard this story before? How could a ghost story be so famous that it found its way into a history textbook but remain a secret from me, the ghost's namesake?

I head up to the computer to do some research. I spend time online every day, usually goofing around on message boards. I love to start flame wars, firing up strangers just for fun. I argue the other side of some issue everyone agrees on, make bizarre allusions and overblown statements, attack people in strange ways—anything as long as I cannot be ignored. Stuff like "Attention, vegetarians: vegetables have feelings too!! Stop the slaughter of innocent radishes!" I just like getting a reaction, I guess. I never engage in the actual fight. That is key. After the first post, I just hang around, watching, waiting, haunting. Like a ghost. A family trait?

I log on to my mail. Oy. A message from Ebony. I should delete it without reading it. I don't want to know what's happening at my old school. Must live in the present. But I open it up. Of course!

hey, will: we miss you. i never realized what a large presence you were. ha-ha! sorry. had to get at least one in there. but, yeah, you should think about coming back. you belong with us. i always had your back. it wasn't fair that they made you feel like you had to choose. it's not your fault you come from a hearing family. we had fun first-day stuff: i tricked a freshman into thinking the teachers' lounge was really a special hangout for freshmen. he walked right in and sat on the couch, started drinking coffee. got detention for a week! ha-ha. you probably have 9 million stories to tell and 10 million public school girlfriends by now. don't forget me! ebony

Why do girls break up with you and then worry that you're missing them? Is it because they're totally unfathomable? Ah, the classic freshman-into-the-teachers'-lounge move. Well, fun stuff has been happening at CHS too, I think. Shoot. I'm famous! I type "Will Halpin" into a search engine:

> **MYSTERIOUSHAUNTINGS.COM:**
> **William Halpin, the ghost of a deaf coal miner also known as "Dummy," has haunted northeastern Pennsylvania . . .**
>
> **COALCORNER: Miner deaths were all too common, including such horrible tragedies as the death of William Halpin, a deaf miner . . .**
>
> **CARBONTIMES.COM/OBITUARIES:**
> **Carbon County, PA. July 9.—William "Dummy" Halpin, a coal miner for Lackawanna Mines, was killed when a mine he was working in suddenly collapsed. His**

body has not yet been recovered. Halpin was unmarried and is survived by his brother Kenneth . . .

Whoa. My dad's name is Kenneth.

On the newspaper's Web site, there is an option where you can request a copy of the original newspaper obituary with a picture and everything. It costs a few bucks, but luckily I have my mom's credit card number memorized. Have my parents intentionally hidden this fact from me? Is he really our relative? I fill in the request. I can't believe it: Will Halpin is a sort-of-famous dead guy.

My parents rarely mention their extended families. On both sides, most are either dead or in Florida—arguably the same thing. From what I am able to piece together—our family tree looking most like a dying sapling—it seems logical that Dummy would have been my grandfather's uncle. The Ken mentioned in the obituary would have been my great-grandfather, Kenneth Halpin Sr.

Why do I have to learn about my own life this way? Personal history found through Google? Traditions passed down on Web pages? While I sit there wondering what it all means, an instant message window pops up on my screen. The name: Smiley_Man3000. Devon starts chatting like we are old friends. Give the guy an *O* for optimism.

Smiley_Man3000: How does the afternoon find you, my good man?

HamburgerHalpin: who talks like that?

Smiley_Man3ooo: My mother is an English teacher, and my father is a policeman. They are very strict!

HamburgerHalpin: do they beat you if you split an infinitive? bust out the tazer each time you forget to capitalize proper nouns?

Smiley_Man3ooo: I believe it's Taser. And no.

HamburgerHalpin: a girl can dream

Smiley_Man3ooo: What?

HamburgerHalpin: whaddayu want anyway?

Smiley_Man3ooo: So, did you hear about Pat's party?

This grabs my attention. Of course it *would* be Pat Chambers who'd have a party that the A.J.'s of the world would get their BVDs in a bunch about.

HamburgerHalpin: i don't hear anything, remember?

I press Enter, letting the message sit there for a minute. Letting Devon sweat. Even *he* knows more about what is going on at school than I do.

HamburgerHalpin: some people on the bus were talking about it

He must have been typing at the same time I was, because his message appears a split second after I press Enter. It has a carefully placed comma and exclamation point.

Smiley_Man3ooo: Oh, man! Please accept my sincerest apology.

I wait for him to get my second message.

Smiley_Man3ooo: <u>Everybody</u> is talking about it. Pat's dad is renting a hotel. It's going to be a casino theme: roulette, real slot machines, and possibly showgirls flown in from Vegas. It's going to be the most extravagant party ever.

HamburgerHalpin: how the hell is he going to get real slot machines?

Smiley_Man3ooo: You don't know who Mr. Chambers is? He runs casinos. He set up a bunch of them out west before moving here. He's part of the cabal that's trying to open up casinos out by Summit Hills. I'm surprised you didn't hear about it.

HamburgerHalpin: i don't hear anything, jerkface

He apologizes again. Then something clicks from before: A.J. said, "Playing card in his playing face."

HamburgerHalpin: of course i knew all that, and you get a playing card when you get invited

Smiley_Man3ooo: Precisely! There are 52 invitations exactly. Like 52 cards in a deck. People would kill for one of those cards.

Devon could kill all fifty-two people and still not get invited to clean up after the party. He has as good a chance of getting a playing card as I do. Which is about as good a chance as me getting invited as one of the showgirls. Which is too bad, because I can really fill out a halter top. Sexy.

I sign off without saying good-bye, feeling somewhat satisfied that my questions were answered. Maybe Smiley_Man3000 is good for something after all. . . .

CHAPTER TEN

"Who is Will Halpin?"

I ask Mona this question the moment she comes in the front door. (Note: Sign language doesn't translate like regular speech. For example, there is no past tense. I must always live in the present. But I hooked you up. You're welcome. Please send checks. Interpreters make, like, fifty bucks an hour. You know where to find me.)

Mom gives me a confused, head-tilting look and begins fumbling with her satchel-type thing and the two coffee mugs she is carrying. My mother is an angular woman, with a constantly worried expression on her narrow face. She looks even more frazzled than normal when I greet her this way. It's not that she doesn't understand. She is very good at sign language, the result of years of long hours studying with me and a few months of intensive training one summer at Camp

Arrowhead, where I was the only kid rooming with his mommy.

A second later Dad is right behind her. They've been carpooling ever since she hired him at the insurance company. I hate to admit it, but he looks just like me. He is round with the same big baby blues and the annoyingly ironic (in my case anyway) oversize ears. He is heavily bearded and not deaf, although he pretty much lives in a little cocoon anyway. He hardly ever says anything.

"What?" Mom asks. You need both hands for this sign, so she just gives up and drops her stuff. She knows I prefer sign language, so she never makes me read her lips, even though it would be easier for her.

"Who is Will Halpin?" I repeat.

"Wow," she says. "They have you doing some heavy studies in that school. Is this from a philosophy class? Who am I? What does life mean? Things like that?"

"It's from history," I answer bluntly, slapping my fingers.

She gives me her extraquizzical wrinkly eyebrow face.

"I do not follow," she says. There are several different signs for "history," so I try another. Dad is trying to keep up, but we are using words like "philosophy" that don't come up very often. He never attended Camp Arrowhead. He heads into the kitchen, presumably to drown his sorrows in ice cream. It is another thing we share.

I motion for her to come over. My finger jams into the paragraph, leaving a little indentation in the offending page. I poke the words "Dummy Halpin" over and over again. Dummy Halpin. Dummy Halpin. Dummy Halpin.

"Ken," she says, calling to my father in the kitchen, "would you look at this?"

After a second Ken comes in, double-chocolate swirl dripping from his beard. I have no idea what he says because his mouth is full and he's always mumbling.

Mom turns her back to me, presumably to fill him in. I grunt.

"Do not turn your back on me," I sign to her when she returns to face me.

"Sorry, it is just . . . I do not . . . ," she says. And then she stops. Dad mechanically spoons ice cream into his hairy mouth, gazing off into the unknown. "I don't know who this is."

Dad stares at the page, reading the short paragraph. It takes him forever to do anything. He looks up at me with a smile. He does a sign everyone knows: that thing where you make a circle motion with your finger while pointing to your head. Crazy. It *is* crazy.

"What do you know about this?" I ask.

She shrugs. "He's not your grandfather. Maybe an uncle?"

"Can't we learn more?" I ask.

"Let it go," she says. "Don't go digging up ghosts."

But I don't want to let it go. I want to dig up every ghost.

Dad gives me a conspiratorial look. Maybe he knows something more?

"Can I go to the library? Do some research?" I ask. Normally, a parent would love that, right?

"It's getting dark," she says, making a scared face as she shades her eyes from the light.

I make the face that means "So what?"

"It is not safe. It is our job to protect you," she says.

When she does that, makes that sign for "protect," holding her hands up, warding off an unseen enemy, I get pissed. I am so *tired* of being protected. It isn't just the stupid library. It isn't just stupid Dummy Halpin. It's everything unspoken in my whole silent life. I feel my face go bright hot. I storm downstairs to my room. I slam the door behind me over and over again, hoping the noise hurts their damn ears. And then, to prove how seriously irked I am, I go to bed without any dinner.

CHAPTER ELEVEN

It is about 1:30 a.m. I am wide awake. And starving. What was I thinking? I tiptoe to the kitchen for a snack. Mom has saved that night's dinner, lasagna, on a plate wrapped in tinfoil. She even wrote a note: "You're the only Will Halpin for us!" The *i* in "Will" was dotted with a smiley face. I *really* love lasagna, but I can't eat that just on principle. Instead, I eat a weird dinner of cheese slices, cashews, salt and vinegar potato chips, and heaping handfuls of chocolate chips. Then I try to go back to bed, but my stomach is unsteady, and more than that, my brain is itchy. I try counting sheep, deer, cows, and every other stupid animal I can think of. The bovines get spooked, haunted by a coal-smeared Dummy Halpin laughing in the darkness.

I lie on my side, staring at the sick blue glow of my giant alarm clock. It's huge—a special industrial "alarm clock for the deaf" (it actually says that on the box) that shines a bright light and literally shakes you awake in the morning.

So restless. I think about sneaking up to the computer room, spending some time online, maybe haunting some message boards, taunting a few environmentalists or religious conservatives or religious environmentalists, but, no, I need to move. Nothing crazy, just a walk. To watch. To haunt. Be ghostly.

I know it will be risky to sneak out, but at least I have an easy escape route. My basement bedroom has a half window above my bed, just big enough to slide out of. It opens easily from the inside. I worry that it might make a noise when I pop the rusty latch, so I wait after prying it ajar, give Mom and Dad a few minutes to come check on me. I'll just tell them I need some air if Mom comes down in her pink robe or Dad saunters down in his matching blue one. But there comes no terry cloth sentry. Ten minutes tick (another offensive term) by on my alarm clock. I pull myself out of the window quick like a cat (or pretty darn rapidly for a fat bear), thrilled to feel the fresh air in my lungs. I keep one eye on the house, checking for lights flicking on or the panicky sweep of a flashlight. Nothing. I proceed, with no real idea where I am headed, out into the night.

It is misty and cool. The streetlights are a waste of electricity, pointless Q-tips of fuzzy light eaten by the fog well before reaching the ground. It is, I think, not unlike a ghost town. I walk across the yard, careful to avoid our gravel driveway. A stupid conversation about this driveway comes to mind.

"Why do we have the only unpaved driveway in town?" I had once asked in a friendly way. "What, are we stuck in the

1800s?" In fact, we *are* sort of stuck in the 1800s—our house is an ancient farm cottage in a little swath of town as of yet untouched by the modernizing influence of big homes and new money.

Dad had looked away, all nervous. "Why?" I repeated. "Why?"

"Just tell him, Ken," my mother said.

"I . . . like . . . sound," my father had said.

Oh.

After a second I realized he meant "I like *the* sound," and that he wasn't rubbing in loving the entire concept of sound for no reason. Still, why would I get mad at that? I don't care that he likes the sound of his gravel driveway. That's great. He should like *something*. He never gets me. He never gets what might make me crazy and what is no big whoop. This might be partly my fault. But screw him anyway. What does he know about Dummy Halpin? Why does he let Mom bully him? Bully both of us?

I cross the yard, avoiding the apparently mellifluous gravel, staying in the grass. I doubt he'd appreciate the sound of his son sneaking out at two in the morning.

I don't get spooked by noises, don't care about creaky doors, can't be startled by hissing cats lurking in the shadows. There are ways that what makes you different makes you stronger, I think, quoting some half-remembered Arrowhead counselor. I will use what makes me different to be a better deviant!

Not that I am doing anything criminal. Just walking. Just walking alone with my thoughts. Will Halpin is a lonely hunter.

And I know that Mom worries about me, wants to protect me, et crapera. For my whole life, she was always afraid something bad was going to happen to me, which was funny, because it already did and there was nothing anyone could have done about it. Knowing that there were others makes it clear it's just a genetic fluke in our family line. It skips some generations, hits others a little, and hammers others hard. I was born with "problems with my ears" that got worse over time until there was no more getting worse to be done.

But why couldn't they tell me about Dummy Halpin? I imagine the scores of reactions during tomorrow's history class. "Check out the freak, descendant of dead, deaf Dummy. . . ."

I walk faster, trying to shake Dummy out of my head. Then I start running. Just a little jog, not too fast. It's been a long time since I ran, and in a minute or two, my chest and legs are sending queries to my brain. "What the hell are you doing? We don't run." But the pain feels useful. It makes it hard to concentrate on anything else. I stay on the sidewalks, of course, just like when I was a kid. Mom *always* insisted on sidewalks only. Safe for those unable to sense cars. God, they were always trying to keep me safe, safe, safe. I make the wide turn, run defiantly not on the sidewalk but smack-dab in the middle of the street. Feels good.

I round the corner back onto my street and start sprinting toward home, sweating and swearing the whole way. And then I see it, a block from my house, like a recurring nightmare that never goes away. That sign. I remember when I was little and I finally realized that I was the only one who had such a sign. I really used to think that everyone had one: REDHEADED CHILD AREA, TALL CHILD AREA, LEFT-HANDED CHILD AREA, MY DAD'S A JERK CHILD AREA.

I am charging directly at the sign. I run and throw my considerable heft against the metal post. This hurts like hell, but to my surprise, it sways like a tree in a gale-force wind. I back up and survey the damage.

I sign something appropriately nasty at the sign. Then I take a few steps back and charge a second time, and the post snaps clean in two! I stare dazed at a rusty streak on my white T-shirt. I wish it was blood, wish I had punctured my damn skin. I look at my vanquished foe lying broken like a corpse on the battlefield. And I feel pretty damn fine about it.

Suddenly I look around. In my might and fury, I had forgotten that any one of several neighbors could be roused. No lights flicker on, and though my heart beats the palpitations of the paranoid, I think I am undetected.

The sign has snapped near the bottom, leaving just a one-foot rod sticking out of the earth and a lengthy piece of post still affixed to the sign. I want it. But how will I get it in my little window? What will I do with it? The only tools I have are my bare hands. These, and my hate, make me strong. I grab the sign like a throat. I stomp on the post and begin shaking it, bending it slowly at first and then wildly, quickly, until the metal becomes hot from the force. With each turn, it becomes looser and softer and easier until—boom—it pops off from the post like an old dandelion flicked by a careless thumb.

My trophy.

I pick up the metal sign and happily begin to carry it home, as proud as King Arthur brandishing Excalibur. After a few steps, my leg hurts and my shoulder throbs from being used as a battering ram. But I still feel great. I crawl back in the window, carefully placing the DEAF CHILD AREA sign behind me, then stash it under the bed once I'm all in. Sleep comes quickly.

CHAPTER TWELVE

On the way to homeroom, I sleepwalk down the hall, bleary-eyed and unnoticed as always. Suddenly I feel an urgent tap on my left shoulder. The sensation of human contact is so foreign that my first thought honestly is that a bird has mistaken me for a perch. I spin around, ready to fight. It's no bird. The shoulder toucher is about five foot five and has an unmistakable film of nacho dust around his lips.

I scowl, trying to indicate via facial expression the sentence "Are you trying to give a fat kid a heart attack, Devon Smiley?" I'm pretty sure I do a good job conveying this, but I probably could punch him in the face and it would fail to register.

"I heard about the crime last night," he says. There are two things about this revelation that shock my sleep-deprived brain. First of all, he said it in perfectly fluent sign language. None of his letter-by-letter torture. The second is obvious enough. My heart starts to pound, and I feel my face go instantly from china white to deep scarlet.

"What crime?" I ask him, answering his signs with one of my own.

He looks dumbfounded and then repeats, "I heard about the crime last night." Of course he hadn't really learned sign language overnight, just one phrase.

"W-H-A-T?" I ask him again, in his usual way.

"M-Y D-A-D T-O-L-D M-E A-B-O-U-T T-H-E S-I-G-N A-T Y-O-U-R H-O-U-S-E."

I feel like I might pass out. His father is a cop!

"P-E-O-P-L-E I-N T-H-I-S T-O-W-N A-R-E J-E-R-K-S," he says. I nod in agreement. They sure are. Wait, what? "W-H-Y W-O-U-L-D S-O-M-E-O-N-E T-E-A-R D-O-W-N Y-O-U-R S-I-G-N?" he asks.

Before I can answer, he gestures for me to follow. Second bell for first period must have already rung. As we walk to class, he gets excited, remembering something.

"S-O Y-O-U A-R-E F-A-M-O-U-S!" Does he really think that having a sign torn down makes me famous? Then he points to the textbook and signs with a big smile, "W-I-L-L H-A-L-P-I-N!" I slap myself on the forehead.

I rumble into my seat in history, and Smiley's ponytail retreats to his spot in the back. It is weird that the police already heard about the "crime" of the DEAF CHILD AREA sign but reassuring to know that they thought it was someone just being a jerk. I set aside that worry for a different one, which was actually an old one (well, a day old anyway). Is everyone in class going to be whispering about Dummy Halpin in the book and laughing about the fact that they are classmates with a ghost's relative?

I scan the class, waiting for Arterberry to take center stage. No one seems to be paying me undue attention. Maybe I am like my namesake, just not technically dead? The class chatter, inasmuch as I can gather, is about Pat Chambers.

"Oh my God! Did you hear?" Mindy Spark blurts to a group of people who only seem to be half paying attention. "Pat's dad was on the news this morning." Her audience remains steadfastly unimpressed. "The *national* news, you guys." This raises a few eyebrows, gets a few heads nodding.

Even Chuck Escapone opens his eyes and looks around with a smile—the equivalent of anyone else screaming at the top of their lungs.

"He *is* so cool, you guys!" Mindy adds. "Seriously."

Pat hasn't arrived yet—he likes to stroll in a few minutes after the bell every day just because he can—but I know Mindy is saying this for her own eventual benefit. She is clearly lobbying, hoping that he will observe her being well informed about all things Chambers and give her a playing card.

Arterberry finally shows up, looking a little weary, like maybe he too was up all night attacking traffic signs.

"How did you (*something something*) the reading?" he asks. I start to sweat. It is officially time to face the ghost of Dummy Halpin. It is time to watch as my classmates make light of my family history, my deafness, my freakish forerunner. But at that moment, Pat walks through the door. Most eyes are on him. Mindy waves. Leigha gives him a hard-to-read look. What is up with her eyes? Only Devon acknowledges me, giving me a huge thumbs-up from across the room. Can I crawl under my desk? Hmm . . . A bit too much of me for that.

"Was there anything (*something something*) found interesting?" Arterberry asks. I am getting better at reading his lips, but I am beginning to wonder if *he* even did the reading. But then he says, "Anything that relates to our class?" turns toward me, and gives me a wink. "How about (*something something*), Mr. Carlson?" he asks. Poor D.C. adjusts his glasses and speaks with his eyes down as if reading his notes, even though he is obviously totally making it up as he goes along, saying something like: "The history of coal mining is important to our class because it is an important part of our region of Pennsylvania. Coal is something that was mined for many years, the mining of which was used for many things. In conclusion, coal mining was—"

Arterberry cuts him off with a raised hand and a withering look. I am beginning to feel relieved. Is it only Devon and I who have done the reading? Arterberry then turns and looks straight at me.

"Didn't any of you (*something*) the reading at all?" He is exasperated, not surprised, and maybe a little sad. I find myself feeling bad for him. I look around the room. Only Devon's hand is raised. I have no choice but to also raise mine. The rest of the class keeps their arms down, so it looks like we are waving at each other. Then he actually does wave to me. *Hi, Devon!* Arterberry is not amused. He does not want to call on Devon. He clearly wants to call on me but does not know how. I *could* speak. I could say a few words, make the sad bastard happy. But my voice makes people laugh. Arterberry stares at me and then pretends I said something.

"Thank you, Will," he says. "I can imagine that it was very interesting to you. The rest of you (*something something*) should know what I mean. Was the miner in the text related to you?" he asks me. I nod my ever-reddening head. "I (*something*) you knew that story?" I shake my head.

"See that, class," he says, waving the book. "You should try reading; you might learn a thing or two." Then he explains that "our Will Halpin" is named for a famous coal miner, which is something "anyone could be proud of deep inside." I feel something deep inside, but I think it's nausea and maybe . . . shame?

CHAPTER THIRTEEN

When I get to Miss Prefontaine's room (a little late due to my routine of following Leigha Pennington . . . but I'm *not really* a stalker), The Dolphin is nowhere to be found. Word has already spread that we have a sub for the day, so plans are no doubt made to make his life miserable. We used to do some classic stuff to the subs at the deaf school, especially the hearing ones. We'd sign outrageous filth with happy smiles or make epic mouth farts when the sub turned around to face the board.

All Travis Bickerstokes and Pat Chambers, the leaders of this classroom, can think of doing is making people switch seats. Pat takes Travis's chair with a big grin. Marie Stepcoat is absent, so they bully Devon into her chair. Devon, being Devon, clearly doesn't want to engage in such tomfoolery, but Travis whispers some sort of threat that gets him to reluctantly play along. He sits there obviously upset about breaking the rules.

The sub enters—a big bruiser of a man with one angry eyebrow and meaty fists clenched tight. He says his name, but I don't catch it and decide to call him MTG (for Mr. Tough Guy). He looks at the seating chart and takes attendance. When he calls Pat's name, Travis says, "Here." Pat loves it. MTG says, "We say, 'Here, sir,' son," which Pats also finds really hysterical.

The rest of the roll proceeds normally until MTG gets to Marie's seat. He looks at the seating chart, then up again, back and forth. He catches on.

"I take it that you are Marie Stepcoat, little lady," he says.

Devon nods and smiles a sad smile. MTG flips the lights on and off, a weird move that is presumably supposed to make us calm down. Then he does a quick bit of math and sees that there are only two boys left who haven't had their name called yet. A big vein throbs in his fat neck.

"Now, I see here that you must be Devon or Will," he says. He grunts something through gritted teeth that I can't make out. Devon says his name, quickly adds "sir," and scampers back to his own seat.

"So you must be Will," MTG says to me.

I nod.

"We say, 'Here, sir,' " he says again, or something like that. His mouth is a thin and angry fault line over a dangerous earthquake. He is about to blow—a bottle of Diet Coke loaded with Mentos.

I debate my options. They are few and crappy. Maybe just doing some sign language at him would make the point?

"MTG," I begin, "your lack of cleavage saddens me." (Might as well have some fun, right?) I do the signs with a serious and respectful look on my face. But, yup, he thinks I am pranking him. That I am a normal kid. Boy, is he wrong.

"Very funny, fella," he says. "Now you say, 'Here, sir'!" I can tell that he is screaming and note how the class is starting to stir. Then Devon Smiley comes to my defense.

Devon cringes the whole time like MTG really might hit him or something. I can't see what he is saying.

"Sorry, kid," MTG says to me, with something actually re-sembling a smile. Devon must have been really convincing.

"You are not forgiven, evil MTG," I sign.

"That means 'I'm sorry, and I'm here, sir,' " Devon says.

I nod.

With the roll finished, Mr. Tough Guy seems to think his role as educator is well and verily done. He announces that Miss Prefontaine left worksheets for us and that we should shut our mouths and use our brains for once. Good and apt teacherly advice.

I write a note asking if I can go to the library. MTG seems unsure what to do. He looks at the paper like a bank teller get-ting a stickup note. But then he just shrugs and lets me go. So there.

CHAPTER FOURTEEN

The library proves to be a nice refuge. I like the quiet. (That's a joke.) And the computer network. They have all sorts of firewalls and filters, but you can get around them if you are a genius like me. (That's a joke too. Actually, I'm no genius, but I'm not the complete opposite of one either.)

I am online and filter-free in just over a minute, logging on to my mail and then researching a question on the Web. Mindy Spark's comments have, uh, sparked my curiosity. Why would Pat Chambers's father be in the national news? One problem: I don't know Mr. Chambers's first name. I take a shot that his is the sort of family where kids are named after their fathers and type "Pat Chambers" into the search box. There are way too many hits, including the faculty page of one Professor Pat Chambers, PhD in endocrinology. Hmm . . . Seems unlikely. I add "Pennsylvania" to my search and find two promising leads.

The first is a pesonal Web page; the second is a "news alert" at CNN.com. Pat's dad is indeed the famous Pat Chambers Sr. I follow the link to the news alert. I read the article, copying the key points into my notebook:

CORRUPTION IN CONGRESS

Businessman and casino owner Pat Chambers Sr. of northeastern Pennsylvania was subpoenaed today to testify in front of Congress as part of the ethics investigation into Senator Harry "Skip" Laufman, R–New Mexico. Laufman is charged with issuing gambling licenses in return for political favors and campaign contributions. Chambers is likely to be asked to explain his business relationship with Laufman. There are allegations that he gave lavish gifts to Laufman to ensure that his company was granted a gambling license.

Chambers operated six casinos in New Mexico and Oklahoma before moving to Pennsylvania, where he now lives and is currently lobbying for several new casinos. Chambers is facing fraud charges as well in a separate federal investigation set to go to trial later this year. If he is found guilty, construction of these projects would be put on hold and Chambers could face federal prison as well as fines reaching into the millions.

I am somehow at once shocked and completely not surprised. Pat's Dad *would* be involved in some slick-and-greedy business deals. And of course suck-ups like Mindy Spark would miss the whole point of the news story and just get excited because "Pat Senior was on TV!" So, Pat Chambers Sr. is a professional scumbag. Like father, like freaking son.

Sufficiently riled, I decide to check out the other search result: Pat Chambers's Web page. It has all of the normal stuff you'd expect: thousands (literally, thousands) of "friends," smirking pictures of Pat (looking drunk), cliché answers to dumb questions (*Fav music?* "A little bit of everything." *Describe yourself:* "I'm a regular teenage guy"). Fascinating. And then under "personal homepage" there is a link to something called ChamberMaids.com. Above the link it indicates the last update (about a week and a half ago), alongside the headline "Check Out the Newest *Addition* to the List." OK. I will.

Only, if you don't have the password, a little box pronounces itself "sorry 4 u, suckah." But I am pretty sure this suckah can guess the content. I've read about this, sleazy guys making online shrines honoring all the girls lucky enough to "date" them. Nasty pictures, sordid stories, lurid details, creeps who drug girls and film them. I start thinking about different tricks for hacking passwords. For example, you'd be shocked how many people just leave the default or do something truly dumb like "123" or "asdf." Knowing a bit about the person helps too. The name of a pet, a birthday, predictable stuff. Sometimes it's their favorite thing in the whole world, which means in this case probably a simple "PAT."

Before I have a chance to try, however, a window pops up over the page.

Smiley_Man3ooo: How does the day find you, my good man?

HamburgerHalpin: hey aren't u still in math?

Smiley_Man3ooo: Yes, sir.

HamburgerHalpin: i don't get it

Smiley_Man3ooo: I'm on my handheld. It rules. It's a Crony. You can get online easily. The weirdo sub just let us have a "free period." I was sort of sad that we'd be missing The Dolphin today, but it has turned out OK.

I don't really want to respond with any discernible enthusiasm, but I have to.

HamburgerHalpin: i'm jealous. cronys r awesome. oh, & thanks for before. you know for explaining me to mr tuff guy

Smiley_Man3ooo: No problem, my good man. No problem at all.

HamburgerHalpin: so what were u talking about b4? oh and good work learning those signs

Smiley_Man3ooo: Thank you! There's some good Web sites out there. Videos and everything.

HamburgerHalpin: u r like an old pro

Smiley_Man3ooo: Great! I have had an interest in signing for quite some time. I taught myself the alphabet last summer--I like to challenge myself between semesters.

HamburgerHalpin: nerd alert

Smiley_Man3ooo: Hey!

HamburgerHalpin: sorry continue

Smiley_Man3ooo: What I was talking about was the DEAF CHILD AREA sign near your house. It got torn down. Did you notice?

HamburgerHalpin: no no i didn't

Just because I am feeling a little friendlier toward Smiley_Man3000 doesn't mean that I want to reveal my criminal past.

Smiley_Man3ooo: Yeah, it did. I'm really sorry.

HamburgerHalpin: i don't get it. i didn't even notice it got torn down. how did u hear?

Smiley_Man3ooo: My father works for the police department. He told me.

HamburgerHalpin: that's right. i knew yr dad was a cop

Smiley_Man3ooo: He's not actually a cop. He used to be a patrol officer. Some wanker named Hawley had a beef with him, and now my dad, who is a great cop, gets stuck doing stuff like checking in stolen property or dispatcher work. He was on the radio on the overnight/early-morning shift last night.

HamburgerHalpin: wait, someone called in the sign being down? what is it with this lame town? what would people do if something real happened? who was it? my mom?

Smiley_Man3ooo: I want to say the Finkbeiners? My dad said they call a lot.

HamburgerHalpin: Finkelsteins?

Smiley_Man3ooo: That sounds right.

HamburgerHalpin: they r my neighbors

Smiley_Man3ooo: That would explain it.

HamburgerHalpin: she's always giving nasty looks

Smiley_Man3ooo: Why's that? You seem to be a perfectly likable chap.

HamburgerHalpin: we had a torrid affair and it ended badly. she's super bitter

Smiley_Man3ooo: Really?!?

HamburgerHalpin: u r 2 gullible. plus you use words like chap and good man way 2 much

Smiley_Man3ooo: Sorry.

HamburgerHalpin: i'm just kidding around

Smiley_Man3ooo: I knew that.

HamburgerHalpin: right sure you did

Smiley_Man3ooo: I did!

HamburgerHalpin: you totally thought i had a love affair with my 8oo-year-old neighbor

Smiley_Man3ooo: Did you mean to type "8o"?

HamburgerHalpin: i stand by what i said

Smiley_Man3ooo: She's really 8oo?

HamburgerHalpin: 8o1 next bastille day

Smiley_Man3ooo: Wow, you like 'em wrinkly.

HamburgerHalpin: smileyman r u teasing me?

Smiley_Man3ooo: Sorry.

HamburgerHalpin: it's cool. funny. especially because it is actually you who loves old lady saggy boobs!

Smiley_Man3ooo: Do not!

HamburgerHalpin: u <3 || (.) (.)

I crack myself up with this one. He doesn't respond for a while, though. Maybe the connection has gone bad? Then the message comes back as this:

> Smiley_Man3ooo: omg. oh i love u and i totally want to be yr boyfriend! I LOVE DUUUUDES!!!!!!!!!!

Several things about this are clear: The first is that Devon does not love dudes. The second is that somebody in class hijacked Devon's Crony, read our chat, then added their own message. They must think this is the height of hilarity. Wait. Do they know it is me on the other end? Do they see my name on there? Are they swift enough to figure out who Hamburger-Halpin is? I scroll up and see that nowhere does it actually say my real name, so maybe I am safe. I don't want my swim trunks, or my life, to be flushed down the toilet. Too much of a splash for Watcher Guy.

CHAPTER FIFTEEN

Lunch today: hot dogs, some sort of broccoli casserole thing, and . . . an apple? It is unnatural to eat anything green, and apples are just pointless. Seriously, what am I, a horse? A pig? Don't answer that. While wolfing down several hot dogs, I spy with my little eye A. J. Fischels sitting angry and more or less alone on the fringes, far from his usual group. Even Gabby Myers has abandoned him and is squeezing into a seat a few tables over with Teresa Lockhart.

Must not get caught staring at A.J. again. Then, ah, the random universe smiles on me, because, just as I begin my search, the most beautiful girl in school sits clearly in my line of sight. Leigha Pennington. I don't get to use the word "gorgeous" very often, especially since I can't quite remember the sign for it. (I do know the sign for "good-looking"—you just point to your own face. Our signing forerunners must have been a vain lot.) But "gorgeous" is the only word for Leigha. Words like "pretty" or "hot" just don't cut it. I guess every school has a Leigha, and ours is Leigha.

Today, in very un-Leigha fashion, she is alone. I contemplate smiling at her or waving or even passing a note. Maybe Leigha is lonely too, at least for this one tiny moment? But, no, of course not. In less time than it takes for me to swallow a hot dog, she pulls people into her orbit without even trying. Pat Chambers comes over to her side and gives her a little kiss on the cheek that she seems disgusted by (maybe, I dare to hope, we share a mutual revulsion for the odious P.C.—wishful thinking?). They don't exactly look like a couple in love. She pulls back from his touch and stares at the dirty floor.

Purple Phimmul slides in next to her and starts patting her hair, an oddly sweet gesture. D. JONKER hovers in the background. And then the iron anvil head of Travis Bickerstokes drops in the seat across from my Leigha, effectively turning the channel on the only good thing to watch.

I continue to stare at the back of Travis's head, just sort of zoning out on his bristly haircut and massive ears. I feel like when you're a kid and you drop an ice cream cone on the sidewalk and are just so completely sad, like that ice cream cone is the whole world. Then Pat notices me staring at Travis's head. His eyes light up like he is happy to see me. "Hey, Trav," he says. "Looks like you have a new boyfriend." Travis whips his massive head around and is staring at me eyeball to eyeball from just a few feet away, but he still doesn't see me. He turns back toward Pat.

"That fat deaf kid," Pat says. "I guess (*something something*) his relationship with Devon Smiley isn't exclusive." He then starts telling all of them (yes, including Leigha) about how he caught me and Devon chatting "like two little girls in love."

I want to point out that what he is saying doesn't make any sense. Are we boyfriends or girlfriends? How are two little girls supposed to be in love? What's wrong with texting someone? I am not in love with Devon Freaking Smiley! I am in love with beautiful Leigha Pennington!

But Leigha laughs too, just like all the others. And then Travis comes over to my table, picks up my broccoli casserole, and throws it at me. It only sort of grazes my shoulder, and I didn't want to eat it anyway, but, still, having food thrown at you is rarely a pleasant experience. The one upside of the incident is that it draws the fury of Mr. Yankowski. Old Yanky-Wanky comes flying across the room, a whirling tornado of gleaming scalp and khaki pants.

"Bickerstokes!" he yells, the vein in his neck throbbing like a drum. I don't see the rest of the conversation because I slip behind him, skirt the traffic circle that inevitably forms to gawk anytime something terrible happens, and disappear into the hallway. I calmly walk toward the double doors to the parking lot and am gone.

Poof!

Trees and birds. The warmth of the sun. Sweet-smelling flowers. Cars cruising by, their drivers in their own little cocoons. Maybe I'll just stick out the old thumb. That's one sign that everybody knows. But what then? Where do I want to go?

What if I get picked up by some scurvy perv with icky intentions toward a handsome young lad such as myself? I wish I had my own car, but there's the matter of driver's ed, a class where you need an interpreter, and neither the public school nor the deaf one offers one.

So I just walk. Behind the school grounds, the mountains slope down an ancient, ratty road built to search for coal, always searching for more coal. Up the hill is a barbed-wire patch labeled DANGER, ABANDONED MINE SHAFT: KEEP OUT! From the party rubble (beer cans, condom wrappers, cigarette boxes) stuck in the barbed wire, it seems like maybe everyone *isn't* keeping out. I think about going up there and checking it out, but I'm not exactly a fan of physical exercise, so I walk only as far as seems necessary to escape being caught. I find a patch of surprisingly soft grass on the hill's scarred side. The midday sun filters through the trees, making a twinkling pattern all around. I decide to lie down for a little while and just stare up at the big sapphire sky. I have never skipped school before and have no idea what to do next. Lots of uneasy thoughts flutter inside my head as birds and fat, lazy bees flutter above me. Will Mr. Yankowski notice I am gone? Will Travis seek some sort of revenge? Will I get detention? Electroshock therapy? Tasered?

Who am I kidding? Only Devon Smiley will even register my absence, and he is probably too busy getting his nipples twisted in the locker room by D. JONKER. Jonker has really stepped up his harassment of Devon lately for some reason.

Right now it all seems so far away: gym class, Devon's nipples, Pat, Leigha, Principal Kroener, Fatzy McFatpants.

Suddenly I feel a strong presence. It's hard to explain, but deaf people definitely sense things. I don't hear it exactly, but maybe I smell it? Smell the sound waves? Taste the presence on the air? Something is here, and it is getting closer.

In the split second before I jump up and open my eyes, I have several thoughts: Is it Yankowski tracking me down? Or Travis Bickerstokes? Is he going to beat me senseless for getting him in trouble? Or maybe—and this seems the most likely option, even here in my moment of Walden-like peace—I am to be bothered by Devon Freaking Smiley. Odd thing is, I am quite happy at that thought. Just not in a romantic way.

CHAPTER SIXTEEN

When I open my eyes, it's like when you think that thing on your plate is a cube of cheese and then you bite it and you find out it's actually zucchini. At first your tongue is just totally baffled, and it takes a while for your brain to adjust its preconception to the new reality.

It is a dog—a goofy black-and-white long-haired mutt with a mouth that turns upward into a floppy smile. He ambles over to me like we are old friends. Like it is the most natural thing in the world. And this is so kind that it almost makes me want to cry.

I want to take him home and give him a bath and a great name (maybe FFD, for Friendly Forest Dog, or just Ace because that's a cool cani-name). I'd let him sleep in my room and lick my face, and we'd be best friends. I immediately feel sad, though, even as Ace (he is definitely an Ace) happily wags his tail and stares at me like there is no one else in the world so perfect. I can't keep him. Mom hates dogs. She isn't crazy about cats either. I guess it's the fur or the whole "I don't need another mouth to feed" thing. The only pets I ever had were goldfish, which aren't that fun and also have a bad habit of dying from neglect.

"Well, at least you can keep me company on the walk home," I tell Ace, realizing as I do that it is maybe sort of weird to sign to a dog. I have to get home before Mom and Dad but not too early, what with our neighborhood spy (and my love interest), eight-hundred-year-old Mrs. Finkelstein, keeping watch. Ace follows me. The walk home is bleak and strange. Most of our city is as bland and modern as anywhere else in America, filled with Taco Bells and chemical plants (note: coincidence?), but the walking route I take from school to home shows slices of the past. Half-falling-down buildings—relics of the coal-mining era—are still visible. They hang incongruously in the shadows above the shining new construction, receding into the background. Like ghosts.

I walk past a rusty bridge that retreats into the woods for a few hundred yards, then gets swallowed up by trees and the side of the mountain. A bridge to nowhere is probably symbolic of something in this town, of my life maybe. I read the graffiti that marks the bridge's underbelly. Mostly old band names: Pantera, Metallica, Fugazi, Black Sabbath. I feel very damn sad. There are also declarations of love: "MS + SA." "Kelly is hot." "PC + LP." I feel even sadder. I walk slower and slower, past the old abandoned buildings and slightly surreal constructions sticking out of the scarred earth. FFD follows alongside, stopping from time to time to whiz on the curb or chew on a stick.

"Do not do that in the basement," I sign, realizing that I have made some sort of decision about this dog. He perks his head in that angle dogs do when they are trying to understand. One ear standing straight up and the other flopped over. Then I swear he gives me a little nod. Does this dog know sign language? Or, more importantly, can I *convince* people that he knows sign language? I can pretend that he's my service dog and use it as an excuse to bring him everywhere. He can come to class with me and alert me to when the bell rings. Maybe he can give me a secret signal if one of my farts is audible or I'm chewing too loud in the caf.

I smack my leg, telling him to hurry up. It's getting late, and he's taking another whiz. "Come see your new home," I sign.

CHAPTER SEVENTEEN

I make it home before the parents. At our happy Halpin dinner, I'm a little sweaty and quite a bit nervous, what with having just smuggled a dog into the basement. My biggest concern? Fear that he's going to start barking. I gave Ace a leftover pork chop I found in the fridge (now, that's love), hoping it would keep him busy. I also brushed all the hair off me and look pretty spiffy. So far, so good. Mom is sitting at the table, not noticing anything. Dad, it seems, isn't joining us. I start wondering: If they get a divorce, who would I live with? Will we sell the house? Who will take me to my Little League games and dance recitals? Will one of them feel guilty enough to buy me a car?

Dad is in the garage, apparently intent on spending the entire night out there. He never tinkers with cars or builds shelves like some dads do. As far as I know, he just stares at the wall and listens to his old radio—not exactly a hobby rife with father-son bonding opportunities. Fine with me—I like a quiet meal. That's a joke. I do like meals, though. No joke. Mom is a master in the kitchen. Maybe if she wasn't so gifted, I'd be a thin and dashing young swimming star or something? Perhaps not. But, oh boy, she sure can cook: pies on a nightly basis, Polish delicacies like pierogi and halupki. (Halpin is a British name, I think, but she was a Kowalski before she got hitched to Ken.) On this night, however, the meal is frozen pizza, frozen peas, and frozen garlic bread. It's like a school lunch. I half expect Purple Phimmul to plop in the seat across the dining room table and start yelling about credit limits and shopping, dammit.

"How was school today?" Mom asks like always, a simple, friendly question that has surprisingly complicated answers. Like every kid throughout the history of the world, I answer, "Fine." A total lie.

"Our math teacher was out," I decide to tell her, thinking it is a safe topic. "We did not have to do any math. That was nice."

"Why do you hate math all of a sudden?" she asks. "You used to be very good at it. Remember when you won that math challenge at Camp Arrowhead? Are you going to keep up your streak of getting A's?"

I should have known better.

"We haven't even had a test yet. But I'll probably fail."

Why did I say that?

"Do you want me to get out your report cards?" she says, signing while holding a little piece of pizza in her fingers. "Remind you of all the A's you got in math?" Hmm . . . Seems

Mom's not in a joking mood. But I point to the little bit of pizza in her hand anyway and say, "You should never talk with your hands full." The first time I made this joke, she laughed so hard that she shot soda out of her nose. Granted, I was eight years old then, a cute little butterball cutup, but it is still one of our favorite lines. No reaction tonight, though.

The conversation is clearly going to come around to whether I should really be in mainstream ed this year. Whether I am making progress with the new hearing devices. Whether the headaches have come back.

So what I say is: "Sure, Mom. I would love nothing more than to sit here and look at my old report cards. Exactly the ideal night for a sixteen-year-old boy." And then I think about throwing my peas at her, which should produce a fine dramatic effect. But I just get up and storm off to my room. Then I come right back in, grab another piece of pizza, and storm off again.

Pizza in one hand and my mouse in the other, I don't feel exactly good about what I said to her. Online I select (*not* click) a few bookmarked message boards to see if anyone has taken any of my recent bait. Nope.

The pizza is already gone, and the Internet is letting me down as a source of happiness and renewal. What's a fat kid to do? Go for a jog? An instant message pops up.

Smiley_Man3ooo: Hello!

HamburgerHalpin: hey

Smiley_Man3ooo: How does the evening find you?

HamburgerHalpin: sux

Smiley_Man3ooo: Why is that?

HamburgerHalpin: ur school is hella lame

Smiley_Man3ooo: Where did you used to go?

HamburgerHalpin: deaf school

Smiley_Man3ooo: Why did you leave, if I may ask?

HamburgerHalpin: dumb crap mostly

Smiley_Man3ooo: Such as?

HamburgerHalpin: at the deaf school--everything got so serious. you're either with us or against us. and when people found out i was even thinking about mainstreaming they flipped

Smiley_Man3ooo: Why?

HamburgerHalpin: you're betraying our community, stuff like that

Smiley_Man3ooo: Just because you wanted to change schools?

HamburgerHalpin: yup

Smiley_Man3ooo: Shouldn't it be your choice?

HamburgerHalpin: u make it seem so simple smileyman

Smiley_Man3ooo: Sometimes it is.

HamburgerHalpin: well sometimes it isn't

Smiley_Man3ooo: Hang in there, chap! It is past my computer curfew!

My fingers find their way back to the mouse, then back to the browser icon, then back to another bookmark. They are moving as if on their own toward a page I had been trying to quit like a bad habit. I am in a dysfunctional relationship with someone who doesn't even know me.

Leigha's Web page depresses me, but I still visit it. The first thing about her page that makes me sad: you can't see any of the good pictures unless you are her friend, and even though I've tried under about eight different fake profiles to get her to accept my friend request, she never has.

According to her profile, "Music is the sound track to my life." This is not that deep of a thought, because what else is going to be the sound track to your life? Shut up, Will. Do not make fun of lovely Leigha Pennington. She has very particular tastes and expresses a particular disdain for emo, which apparently is a type of rock or something? (I'm not a big music aficionado.)

Mainly, I just look at her beautiful profile pic. She is wearing jeans and a plain white sleeveless shirt, hair falling down in soft ringlets over her ears. She is smiling a huge smile and hugging a floppy-eared black dog. If you look briefly at the picture, you might think she is happy. But if you look at it for a few minutes (or an hour or two, or maybe a few hundred thousand hours), something else becomes clear. There is a melancholy around her eyes that the world misses, that no one else can see. Except me?

A lyric quoted underneath the pic says, "No one hears the last note of the song / No one appreciates what you have till you're gone. / I'm alone even more than most / An empty shell / A shadow of a ghost." I just know that all she needs is someone to talk to and the weight would be lifted. And since I am the only one who knows it exists, I am the perfect choice. But I can't talk to her, and so we are both doomed, two parallel planets whose orbits will never cross.

I move over to the "friends" area, and I find myself face to face with the unsettling gaze of Purple Phimmul. I dive in. Purple's Web page is a strange experience. At school she's this fascinating foreign object. Online she turns out to be pretty blunt, sharing her life history and inner thoughts with anyone interested in clicking (uh, selecting). They always teach you about online safety and how you shouldn't make your location clear, but Purple is posing right in front of her house, a famous old mansion that anybody who's ever been to town can locate in two seconds.

On Purple's page, the Phimmul blog has some interesting tidbits.

I was born in NYC—don't you forget it! Represent. My parents moved us to Vanilla PA, the land that time forgot. I miss the city (for shopping, yeah, and for everything). It works for now, I guess. Daddy can still make it to work in NY, and plus we have a bunch of family around here. Mom said the move is supposed to "restore some normalcy" to our family. I don't see that happening. How can one restore that which one never had?

There are a bunch of pictures, some in that new dress she got. The caption says something about being a queen at P.C.'s party. She looks happy enough, if a little flabby. Why is she so happy? She's not skinny or pretty—I guess rich trumps all that. Am I envious of the weirdly confident Purple? I mean, yeah, I'd like to be rich. But it's more than that. She cruises around the whole world like it's her living room. I can pretend to fit in (barely), but do I ever belong? Does she even know what it feels like *not* to belong?

I stare at the pictures. She's so fully Purple. You have to give her that. I am too embarrassed to have any pictures online. I even try to get out of family pictures. But there is something very similar about us. And her family is from Pennsylvania too?

I am curious (aka nerdy) enough to do a search on her mansion. There is a local history Web site about it with pictures of her family. One of her ancestors, named Andy Phimmul, catches my eye because he has a big, fancy mustache and an ancient hearing aid. They were called ear trumpets back then. It looks like a small tuba sticking out of his smiling face.

OK, it's getting late. Back to Leigha. Should I send her a message? Maybe I could just reach out to her under a fake name. Just so she knows somebody knows. Or maybe—and here's a wild thought—I could send her a message as . . . myself?

I decide to write it by hand because there is no "save draft" option on this site. I get out my notebook and start composing:

My dearest Leigha,

I rip out this page and throw it away. How about . . . acronyms!

Hey, L.P.

I rip this page out too. I can't even get the first few words out without coming off as totally lame.

Hey, Leigha! What's up?

Better.

You have probably seen me around. I'm the fat deaf guy in the Phillies shirt who people sometimes throw casseroles at.

This too is laid to rest in the wastebasket on top of a pizza-smeared napkin. Is this an impossible mountain I can never climb? And then it comes to me in a flash. A friendly but slightly romantic message that will hit all the right notes, if you will. It will just require that rarest of Halpin emotions: honesty. So I write without really thinking. It is like my hand is moving on its own, channeling these cosmic words:

Hey, Leigha!

This might seem like a strange message, and maybe I'm a strange guy. I'm also, if you get to know me, pretty funny and nice and even an excellent dancer. (OK, I'm lying about that last one.) I'm Will, the deaf dude in a few of your classes. So, yeah, the school could stand some improvements, but I have noticed that you seem like a cool person. I happened upon your Web page (by "happened upon" I mean "did a search for"), and I get the feelin' that we should probably hang out. I can teach you sign language; you can get me up to date on the music scene. And maybe you can tell me if I'm right or just crazy (definitely a possibility) that in your profile pic there is something just a bit sad in the way you are smiling. Maybe things suck a little for you too? Maybe you want to chat about it? Let me know. I'm all ears. (Ha-ha.) —Will Halpin

I sit back and reread the letter a few hundred times. My heart flutters in my chest. It is definitely good. Real good. Next I just have to put my e-mail address (HamburgerHalpin@gmail.com) so she can contact me. But how do I sign off? What do I write before my name? "Yours truly"? Am I eight hundred years old? "Sincerely yours"? What does that even mean anyway?

I check out the rest of her page while I think on it. I find some of Leigha's poetry:

I've been on the straight path,
There's got to be more.
There's tunnels and caves I want to explore.

I've been on the straight path,

There's got to be more.

There's got to be more.

There's got to be more.

OK, maybe she's not a great poetess, my future girlfriend. How to end my note to Leigha? I could write:

Your (future?) friend Will

But that seems a little desperate, even with that question mark to soften the blow.

Peace out, yo

Too weird. Can't decide. I leave it blank. I put the page in my math binder and decide to sleep on it. Will my dreams feature those eyes, so sad, so beautiful? That killer ass?

CHAPTER EIGHTEEN

It is the middle of the night when my light flicks on. "What is that noise?" Mom signs, wiggling her hand by her ear.

"You're asking the wrong guy," I sign. Trying to keep it light. I know what it is, though. Ace is barking. I can feel it. I hid him in the laundry room off to the side of my basement lair and had set my alarm to wake me in the middle of the night to check on him, but I guess he got bored waiting for me.

"It sounds like a dog," Mom signs.

I shrug. Dad joins her at the foot of my bed. He has sleep in his eyes. He gives me a suspicious look and walks toward the laundry area. What was I thinking? Of course they were going to find out. And now I am about to lose my new best friend. Christ, I'm pathetic.

Dad is walking back toward my bed. He has Ace by his side. Mom is gasping, covering her mouth with her hand. Dad points to the dog with a question mark on his face. The gesture means "Care to explain?"

"I have never seen that dog before," I deadpan. I love the sign for "before." You pull your hand back toward you, like you're pressing rewind on life. If only.

Dad walks over to me and plucks a black hair off my sleeve. Evidence. He holds it up, then compares it to Ace's back. Ace thinks this means Dad is going to pet him, and he gets so excited that he spins around in a circle. His tail whacks my nightstand, disrupting my messy stack of books. This spooks Ace, and he starts barking at a wobbling Poe anthology. I am having to reconsider the possibility of Ace becoming a service dog. He is afraid of literature, and his only discernible skill seems to be whizzing on stuff. Oh, and now he's humping my mom's leg. Nice, Ace. Nice. This audition is not going well at all. I clench my jaw.

Then Dad starts laughing. "He likes you," he signs to my mom (an easy sign). Then, to my surprise, Mom starts laughing.

"Or at least my leg," she signs.

"He *loves* your leg," I sign. Might as well join in, even if it is a weird thing to say. Ace keeps smiling, like he's in on the joke. Or maybe he just does love that leg. I know when to strike.

"Can we keep him?" I sign, gripping my fingers tightly as I make the sign.

The parents exchange looks, each raising their eyebrows. I look at them and raise my eyebrows. It's like we're having an eyebrow-raising contest—and I am determined to win! Ace stops humping and raises his eyebrows too. We all laugh. Mom is ready to break! Then she has a bunch of questions for me. Will I clean up after him? Feed him? Walk him? Bathe him? I nod yes. Yes. Yes! She is annoyingly skeptical.

"Every day," I promise.

They give me a look.

"What?" I sign. I know what they mean. I'm not the poster boy for daily exercise. They smile. Ace barks. He's in. He's in!

Dad scratches him on the ear, and we all go back to sleep.

Arf!

CHAPTER NINETEEN

"First order of business," Mr. Arterberry is saying as I try to shake the sleep out of my head and focus on history. "Everyone needs a buddy for the field trip to Happy Memory Coal Mine." *Sheesh.*

I scan the room, watching as pairs of eyes lock in silent agreement like pieces in a puzzle that know instinctively where they belong. Stepcoat and Spark. Chambers and Jonker. Even Escapone and Carlson sign up as buddies, some sort of default twosome in a united front against normalcy. Phimmul and Pennington. Hmm. Interesting. Not Pat and Leigha? Why aren't they buddies? And why couldn't her second choice be yours truly, whose pure-ish devotion is hers for the taking? I've watched the two of them, the way Pat looks at her, licking his lips. He's very animalistic. He's a disgusting beast. Doesn't she see that?

So, where else will my puzzle piece click? Where, oh where, but with Devon Smiley? He gives me a serious look and then a nod and then a smile. I do something with my mouth, maybe a grimace. But it is official. We are coal mine field trip buddies. Just not in a romantic way.

Arterberry is writing out the list of buddies, squinting down his nose at a black binder. Devon walks up and hands me a note. A note? After getting caught chatting the day before, I would have thought he'd be more sensibly paranoid.

Hello, my good man.

I forgot to ask on IM last night where you got to yesterday. Did you decide to skip afternoon classes? I wish I had the guts to try that. (I'd skip gym every damn day.) I had a whole story lined up about how you became suddenly and mysteriously transported away from this galaxy. But no one asked. Weird, huh? Anyway, glad to be your buddy!

Dev

Me and "Dev" Smiley.

I try to focus on Arterberry's lecture. It takes me forever to realize that the one word he keeps saying is "bituminous," which is a type of coal. I pick up "anthracite," another type, more easily. But I keep getting lost. So I go back to the text and lose myself in that world: tough guys doing dangerous work amid fires and explosions and cave-ins. Strikes, murders, sabotage, men shot on picket lines, fighting for their rights in our very backyards. Does any of this flow through my own veins? I try to figure out my connection to this world, but, let's face it, I barely know my place in this classroom. In my own family. In my own self.

I think of my old school for some reason, of the battle lines drawn in the sand, now washed away by the ocean of time. See, Leigha? I'm a poet too. Shit.

CHAPTER TWENTY

Lunch is fried ravioli. It is a strange food that does strange things to my normally ironclad gut. As soon as I eat a piece, I feel it expanding like one of those pills that you put in water and watch as it turns into a sponge dinosaur. I go back for seconds.

Straight ahead in my line of sight is Kevin Planders. Unsurprisingly, he is sitting alone. Possibly because he is a loser, but maybe because he is eating a confusing lunch of ketchup packets and beef jerky.

Shouldn't be so harsh. Planders is just another fellow outsider. Maybe he isn't a bad guy if you get to know him. Sure there is always something unsteady in his large, glassy eyes. And, yeah, there is something not quite right in the way his lips move all the time and his face contorts wildly in response to whatever snuff film is playing in his head. Actually, maybe

Kevin Planders *is* a bad guy if you get to know him. Some people are just crazy, and although I'd like to be a saint and befriend him, I have my own considerable ass to cover.

Purple Phimmul is also in full view and wearing some sort of intricately beaded dress. I lock onto her gaze for a second and am met with an angry glare. Geez. Why so pissy, missy? She looks like she's going to stick her tongue out at me. For some bizarre reason, I find myself winking at her. What the hell was that? She seems to be thinking the same thing because the look on her face is total surprise. Then she starts laughing and turns away.

OK, must move along. What else is on? There's a bit of commotion over at Pat's table. D. JONKER is trying to sit down, and Pat keeps subtly sliding his chair out of reach. He doesn't even look at Derrick, just slides the chair a little to the left, then a little to the right. D. JONKER is smiling at first but then becomes very frustrated and screams something that would have gotten him suspended for sure if he wasn't a member of the defensive line squadron or whatever you call it. (I hate football.) Is this about that party? I jot in my notebook: D. JONKER ON THE OUTS WITH P.C.?

As I write, I look up to see Derrick storm off. Then he lands—right at my table. It is like a meteor crashing onto my deserted island. He doesn't even acknowledge me, however. He just looks right through me, chugging his little jug of milk and chomping his fried ravioli with a clenched jaw. Then, to my shock, he pulls out an AP English book, *Great American Writers*. He spreads it on the table, half under his tray. Is he afraid his friends will make fun of him for reading? I pretend to be still looking in my notebook, but I can see that he's opened to a chapter on Emily Dickinson. Something from one of her poems comes to mind: "I'm Nobody! Who are you? / Are you—Nobody—too?" Then he moves on to Poe's "The Tell-Tale Heart." I suddenly want to tell him about how I totally get that story, about how the DEAF CHILD AREA sign under my bed has been taunting me like a pocket watch under the floorboards. It is a little insane, but I go for it.

"I know exactly how the narrator feels in that story," I write. I float the note over his book. He looks at it like I crapped in his milk carton.

"Dude," he says, "don't write me notes."

We stare at each other for a long moment. For some reason I am not intimidated. Somebody who reads unassigned Poe and Dickinson at lunch just isn't a tough guy, no matter how much he wants to be. We could really be friends, I think. *Dude.* But then the bell, presumably, sounds. I see a sudden mass exodus, and with it the possibility of friendship dissipates into the air. Story of my goddamn life.

CHAPTER TWENTY-ONE

Before we even begin getting changed for swimming, Fatzy comes storming into the locker room. He is brandishing a clear plastic bag that contains something wet and brown and, uh . . . poopish. He holds it up like a lawyer presenting the surprise piece of evidence sure to nail the killer. We all look at it with collective confusion.

"Don't pretend (*something something*) what this is, Smiley," McFatpants says. All eyes go to Devon, who clearly has no idea what Fatzy is talking about.

"Come again?" he says, cocking his head like a confused dog struggling to grasp the commands of a lunatic master. Fatpants then adjusts the bag so its contents become clearer. Ah, a swimming suit. He points, his finger shaking with anger, at the waistband. There, someone, presumably Mrs. Smiley, had written "Devon ☺" in humiliatingly permanent marker.

"Do you know how (*something something*) emergency plumbing services to (*something something*) remove this from the drain?"

So, Devon's shorts clogged up the pipes. The school had to spend a lot of money to get a plumber to fish them out. And now Fatzy is furious—with Devon!

Devon tries posing the logical question: "Why would I flush my own swimsuit down the toilet?"

"Well, then, who did?" Fatzy asks.

Devon pauses. Clearly, he does not want to rat out those actually responsible for the old flag-and-flush. Will someone step up and fall honorably on his sword? Of course not.

"Are you telling me that someone other than you (*something something*) flushed your shorts down the toilet?" Fatzinger asks.

Devon nods.

"And that you have no idea who it was that did this?" Fatzy yells. "Someone pulled off your shorts and flushed them down my toilet without you noticing who it was?"

Devon nods again. And get this! He ends up being the one who gets punished. I am thunderstruck. What is this delusion that makes people think that kids who are good at sports are somehow also blessed with a whole host of other positive traits? It should have been obvious to Fatpants that Pat is constantly torturing Devon.

"I bet you flushed these so you could get out of swimming," McFatpants says. "Well, I hope you're happy, because now you will have to sit on the sideline for a week while the rest of us enjoy free swim."

Fatzy's reasoning is stunning. Why is the punishment for ruining the plumbing the exact thing that the punished wanted anyway? All right, then, time to start flushing my own suit on a daily basis. And maybe my math book, my history book, and my lunch. I'll flush my entire life if I can find a toilet big enough.

"Now the rest of you get changed and quick," McFatpants says. "We've wasted enough time already."

And then, perhaps because of all the talk about toilets, or maybe the fried ravioli, I know I cannot "get changed and quick." My stomach is lurching and diving like a pilot on a kamikaze mission. If I try to swim, the plumber might have to come back to drain the entire pool. What to do? Try to explain to this most sensitive of educators, Mr. Fatzy McFatpants, that I am feeling sick to my stomach, and elsewhere?

As I sit on the horn of this particular dilemma (ouch!), I realize I don't have a pen and paper on me. Hmm . . . It is a long shot, but the sign for "diarrhea" is actually pretty vivid: you sort of pull your thumb out of your fist over and over again like your hand is shooting out a turd. I try it on Fatzy, but he just looks confused and really miffed.

Devon is sitting on a bench, pleased to be avoiding gym but shaken up over his dressing-down. He smiles weakly at me. I point to myself and spell "S-I-C-K." I do the sign for "diarrhea" to him, and he gets it. He points to himself and then to Fatzy like he's saying, "You want me to tell him for you?" I nod. It's almost like a real conversation.

Devon skitters up to Fatpants with a scared yet determined look on his face. I have to stop being so hard on Smileyman. Fatpants writes me a pass to the nurse. I smile and scurry down the hall, walking in a butt-clenched crab step inspired by my condition.

As soon as I see Nurse Weaver, I feel panic. It's her job to make sure I'm succeeding at this school. I'm sure she will notice that I'm not wearing my hearing aids. Why didn't I grow one of those floppy hairstyles that would cover my ears?

She gives me a look of tight lips and raised eyebrows. Crap. I've been busted. But she is a kind lady and recognizes the crab walk, so she gives me some Pepto-Bismol and lets me use the toilet in the nurse's office. We'll probably have to have "a talk" about my progress sometime soon. But, for now, there are other pressing matters.

It's possibly sad when a quality crapper is the high point of your day, but this john is really first-rate. There is a padded seat, a little basket of stuff with a sweet smell, and toilet paper that, unlike in the rest of the school commodes, does not seem to be leftover sandpaper from woodshop.

Can I just sit on this toilet all day, maybe actually move in here and make it my house? But wait. What if a line of fellow ravioli eaters has formed at the door? They could be knocking and I'd have no idea. What if they get out a battering ram and knock down the door, thinking I have died, Elvis-style, on the crapper? I finish up and rush the heck out of there. And someone else *is* waiting to use it. A beautiful, sad someone.

Leigha has a sickish green look on her face as she brushes past me to enter the little toilet room. But even while I am sort of worried about the smell I left behind, I feel somehow sure that Leigha and I are destined to make a real connection. So I do the boldest thing I've ever done. And maybe the most brilliant? Or the stupidest?

I take the letter I had written to Leigha out of my binder. Then I take my pen in my hand and, with my heart in my throat, I scrawl "Love" before "Will." Done!

I slide the note under the bathroom door, turn to run, and smack right into Purple Phimmul. The collision almost sends her sprawling to the linoleum floor. Her sunglasses skid across the room. A bead or two flies off of her dress. She struggles to regain her balance, her little sausage-y arms flailing like a T. rex. I pick up her glasses and hand them to her. She plucks them carefully from my sweaty palm like you'd pick a dirty tissue up off the floor.

"Sorry," I sign sorrily. My head is spinning so fast that I forget she has no idea what I am talking about. But then my head spins even faster when she signs something back.

"How did you learn?" I ask.

"Deaf uncle," she responds. "Now I have a question for you."

I signal that she should go ahead and ask.

"What did you put under the door?" Her eyes narrow, and even her hands take on an unfriendly tone.

"Nothing," I sign with shaking hands.

"I brought Leigha down to the nurse because she was feeling sick. I've been sitting here the whole time. I watched you," she signs with really quite impressive sign language.

"It was nothing," I sign again.

She stares at me, her eyes narrowed to slits. Feeling spooked, I just keep making that sign for "nothing," two O shapes exploding into emptiness. And then Purple looks away from me suddenly. Leigha is coming out of the bathroom. And I am running down the hall. Away! Away!

CHAPTER TWENTY-TWO

For the whole rest of the day, I cannot stop imagining Leigha's response to my note. I play out a thousand possible scenarios. I work hard to try to convince myself that the good ones (me and Leigha making out in a shed) are likely, or at least no less unlikely than the really bad ones (me getting murdered in a shed). Why do all these scenarios involve a shed?

Luckily, on the way home, I become distracted by some bus shenanigans. Planders is whooping it up, yelling about how great the football team is and how Pat is the best CHS quarterback ever, yakety-yak. But what I really want to see is at the back of the bus. Gabby is again trying to soothe A.J., who again looks infuriated. And where is Teresa Lockhart?

Is this really all about Pat's exclusive party? Or maybe he is mad because Teresa is off with somebody who is not him? Does he secretly pine for his bus mate? I enter in my notebook: BUS

LOVE TRIANGLE? Burning question. But I have no desire for a repeat of the GAJBF, so I try really hard to keep from being seen.

Should I get some sunglasses like Purple's so no one can see my eyes? Given how little people around here seem to know about being deaf, they might think it would be normal if I wore sunglasses all the time. Would I be the cool "impaired" guy with the shades? Like Ray Charles or Stevie Wonder. Except fat. And white. And not really all that musical.

For now I just have to peek once in a while. I catch some fragments of the conversation. Gabby is trying to keep A.J. from being upset, but it isn't working. The one word I see her say a bunch of times is "ace." Do they somehow know about my Ace? Speaking of which, is he whizzing in the basement at the moment? Nah. But every time I look up, the word "ace" is there as clear as day. What on earth could she be referring to?

I focus as hard as I can and get one long bit of conversation that provides a clue to something I had been wondering about for a while. Something gross.

"Well, maybe you should have known better than to ask Leigha," Gabby says to A.J. "You're lucky all Pat did was take away your invitation. I know they broke up, but he still won't let her go out with anyone else. And, seriously, if anyone so much as texts Leigha, he'll kill them."

CHAPTER TWENTY-THREE

Huzzah. The day of the field trip to Happy Memory Coal Mine has finally arrived. I am so excited that I put on my best outfit, lovingly sculpt my hair, and skip out the front door. Who would not be excited to stand in a dark coal mine with the cretins who make up my history class?

Better and better, Jimmy Porkrinds is our bus driver for the trip. As we cruise up the highway, I amuse myself by copying down what I surmise to be Jimmy's thoughts on life into my notebook: "YOU UNGRATEFUL TURDS. ONE DAY I WILL DRIVE THIS BUS RIGHT OVER A CLIFF!" And then I detect a rumpus in the back of the bus. A group of loyal subjects is encircling King Chambers. He has his arms up on the seat back, a picture of relaxed power.

"I don't know," Pat says. "Maybe I'll take A.J.'s jack and give it to Planders." Several lords and ladies laugh like this is the funniest freaking thing in the world. A.J., now banished to the middle of the bus, sinks farther into his seat. Might he cry?

"No!" chimes in Purple. "Give it to Smiley!" An eruption of laughter. Purple loves her own joke so much that she starts fanning herself like a Southern belle suffering from the vapors.

In the last week, chatter about Pat's fast-approaching party has increased geometrically. From what I have pieced together, the Chamberses are renting the ballroom of a fancy hotel and are having Vegas showgirls flown in. There has been a rumor that the whole reason that hotel was built a few years ago was that Mr. Chambers knew he was moving here and wanted an acceptable place for his son's party. I don't believe this, just like I don't believe that the new football stadium was built just to woo Pat away from the private school across town. But one never knows.

Another hot rumor is that a celebrity DJ is being paid twenty thousand dollars to provide music. I want to say DJ Kumquat—but that can't be it, right? How can it possibly be worth it to pay twenty thousand dollars just so the guy can select the music? The other true-mor, which nobody doubts, is that Pat will get a Lexus or BMW or some obscene vehicle at the end of the night. It's all so annoying. And it's all anyone can talk about.

Even Pat's dad's indictment on corruption charges only adds to the glamour. I've seen him on the news in an expensive suit, handcuffed and getting hauled away as part of the corruption scandal around Senator Laufman. It has to be hard to get arrested for bribing a senator, since it is my understanding that bribery is more common than actual lawmaking down in Washington. Pat Senior apparently went that far beyond business as usual.

In keeping with my CHS duty to stay well informed on all matters Chambers, I spent the previous night online reading up on the case. Some leaked e-mails were posted citing evidence that Mr. Chambers clearly bribed Senator Laufman in order to get a license for his casino and to make sure that all other bids were denied. The competing bidder had already started construction, resulting in a huge loss for them while Pat Senior lined his pockets. All this apparently only adds the sheen of the outlaw to the party, like Pat and his dad are real bad boys being persecuted by the Man.

"Oh no," Pat says. "Smiley's a king o' hearts for sure."

Between Jimmy Porkrinds's psychotic babble up front and this weird discussion in the back, the whole world suddenly seems to make very little sense.

I feel a tap on my shoulder. 'Tis my buddy. We're not allowed to text, even on the bus, so Devon asks me in letter-speak: "W-H-A-T A-R-E T-H-E-Y S-A-Y-I-N-G?"

I guess we are too far away in our front-of-the-bus Siberia for him to hear their conversation. I tell him what Pat said, in painfully slow letter-talk (leaving out the comments about him). Devon grins and tugs on his ponytail.

"I K-N-O-W E-X-A-C-T-L-Y W-H-A-T P-A-T M-E-A-N-S," he says.

Realizing that Purple Phimmul could be watching us and figuring it all out, I hand Devon my notebook. I dig out another pencil from my bag, which also holds the sweater and gloves Mom made me bring even though it is completely warm out. ("It'll be cold in the mine!" she had said. "You sure you don't want gloves? You sure? You sure? You sure?" I gave in. At least she didn't try to pin them to my sleeves.)

I slide the writing tools over to Devon and see that he also has a little bag of warm clothes. Does this make me feel better or worse?

"You want me to write instead of signing?" he writes. Again, he has perfect grammar and also a delicate penmanship style that strikes me as very girlie. I will not put up with any *i*'s with little hearts.

"Yup," I scrawl.

"Remember how we were talking about the casino theme for the bash? And how he's giving out fifty-two invitations?" he writes.

I nod and have to stop myself from making fun of him for using the word "bash."

"Each playing card in the deck has a value, so each invite has a value. Like a hierarchy." He pauses. "Do you know what a hierarchy is?"

"Duh," I write.

"Just asking," he writes. "Sometimes my vocabulary weirds people out."

"I read a lot," I write. "Besides, there are a lot weirder things about you than your fancy-ass vocabulary."

"Hey!" he writes.

"Just kidding."

"The kings and queens are the best. Leigha Pennington is no doubt the queen of hearts. Purple will be a queen too."

Leigha is the queen of my heart. (I can't help myself.) I start thinking about her and feel my stomach lurch as Jimmy Porkrinds pilots the bus around a hairpin turn. Since the whole toilet note thing, she has looked right through me. It's as if I am transparent. And believe me, I'm not.

"Aces are like this wild card he's holding to the end," Devon writes.

So the aces are A.J.'s last chance to get an invite.

"Jacks are pretty desirable too," Devon writes. "I think all the face cards are at the head table. A.J. was going to be a jack, but he ticked Pat off somehow. Get this: I heard Pat joking about giving it to Kevin Planders. Ha-ha."

Pat is assigning values to human beings. Travis is a jack, Leigha is a queen, Gabby Myers would be a solid six, and Devon would be a negative twelve. Can't we all just be tens, like me?

"What are you thinking about?" Devon writes. But before I can answer, I see Pat stand up. All eyes are on him, including Leigha's, whose gaze is burning with a surprising intensity. Even the adults—Porkrinds, The Dolphin, Arterberry, Mrs. Stepcoat (who volunteered to chaperone, to Marie's eyeball-rolling horror)—are watching. Is Pat going to make some sort of announcement?

I feel confident that I can turn around and make no secret that I am reading his lips.

"Attention, ladies and gentlemen," he says. "As you know,

my fiesta is fast approaching. Forty-eight of you have been lucky enough to receive your playing cards. But what of the remaining four? I have been saving four aces, four aces up my sleeve. If you, Will . . ."

I can't believe it! I am getting an ace! I start to stand up. Then Devon gives me a really sharp look and yanks me down. Pat reaches into his sleeve and pulls out four invitations, which look exactly like oversize playing cards. Possibly he was saying "If you will"? Oops.

"The first ace goes to . . . Derrick Jonker! You didn't think I'd forget you, buddy!" Pat starts laughing like this is hilarious.

Devon writes, "Pat kept telling Derrick that he wasn't getting one." The chair. The cafeteria. A kitty playing with his mousie.

Even though he is sitting right next to Pat, Derrick stands up to receive his invitation. He waves to everyone and wipes pretend sweat off his forehead in mock relief. While Travis cracks up, I notice Leigha look out the window. We are passing a farm, and something about the look in her eyes tells me that she wishes she was there, or anywhere, instead of here.

Devon writes, "I knew Jonker would get one!!"

I write, "Duh."

Pat slowly pulls out the next playing card invitation. "The second ace goes to . . . Mindy Spark. Come on over here, Minder." Mindy Spark's eyes open so wide I think they are going to fall out of their overwhelmed sockets. She hugs her seatmate, Marie Stepcoat, who cringes at this horrifying display of enthusiasm.

Mindy composes herself enough so she can make it down the aisle without bursting into flames. She does, however, almost fall over when Jimmy Porkrinds accelerates for no reason at all on a long stretch of open road. Good timing, J.P.!

Mindy literally curtsies to Pat as she accepts her card. I keep sneaking glances at Leigha, who is now looking like she is going to puke. She mouths something, but I can't make out the words. Her lips seem puffy and heavily lipsticked. Did she fall? Was she in a fight?

It takes a lot of energy to not miss a word, but I am getting madder and madder. I write another note to Devon: "Did you see in history class the other day when Spark was telling everyone how cool Pat is and how his dad is 'way famous'?"

"Totally low-class to campaign," Devon writes back, but he is distracted as he writes, looking past me to the back of the bus to see how the rest of the ceremony plays out. Does he wish he had launched a full-scale campaign? Am I any better?

"Now for the third ace . . . ," Pat says, pausing for dramatic effect. "(*Something something*) age over beauty?" he asks. What? "Well, what if someone has both? To make sure that the party is educational as well as a blast, the third choice goes to our mistress of math, Miss Prefontaine."

I am pretty sure that a stunned silence is sweeping the bus. Heads swivel from Pat to Prefontaine. Quizzical glances are shared. Giggles are stifled.

"We have to have a chaperone," Pat says, winking. "Come get your ace, Claire."

Miss Prefontaine is blushing, embarrassed, yet obviously

excited. I try to check Leigha's reaction, but she has turned her head and buried her face in her hands. My poor baby.

Pat gives the ace to Derrick, who walks it over to "Claire." She clutches it like it's a rare and delicate flower. Mrs. Stepcoat looks appalled. Mr. Arterberry is sort of giggling but then composes himself and forces a disapproving glare.

Before the impact of this improbable choice sinks in, without a pause or dramatic speech or anything, Pat holds up the final card and says, "The fourth and final ace goes to Chuck Escapone."

Escapone, zoning out with his headphones on, has to be jostled awake by his default trip buddy, Dwight Carlson. At first he seems annoyed and confused, like a napping toddler startled out of slumber. Then Dwight explains what is going on, and Chuck grins and in true Escapone style actually climbs over the seats in giant, loping steps. Why would Pat choose Escapone for the final card?

I shield the page in my notebook from Devon. This is just for me: (1) DOES PAT KNOW ESCAPONE CAN BE COUNTED ON TO BRING THAT CERTAIN SOMETHING SURE TO MAKE THE PARTY EXTRA-PHARMACEUTICALLY-SPECIAL (AND I'M NOT TALKING ABOUT HIS SPARKLING PERSONALITY)? OR (2) DID PAT INTENTIONALLY PICK THE WEIRDEST PERSON HE COULD THINK OF TO MAKE IT CLEAR TO A.J. HOW FAR HE HAS FALLEN? Hey, with that logic at work, maybe Devon and I were closer to being invited than we thought! If spiting A.J. was the goal, we might have honestly been considered. And isn't that the true unspoken story of the ace ceremony? That A.J. has *not* received an invitation? I reread my notes on the subject, tapping my pencil in thought. Just a few weeks ago, they were something like best friends, and now Escapone is laughing with an ace in his hand while A.J. stares out the window at the sign indicating that the coal mine is a quarter of a mile ahead.

Jimmy Porkrinds takes about a quarter of a second to go a quarter mile, and so we are there in the blink of an eye. Let the Happy Memories begin.

CHAPTER TWENTY-FOUR

The first weird thing that happens at Happy Memory Coal Mine is this: Jimmy Porkrinds is coming on the tour! Did his pod parents have to sign a permission slip? After the back-of-the-bus cool kids depart, Jimmy Porkrinds hops off like a happy field tripper. He just closes up the bus and joins the end of the line, waiting patiently with his hands in his pockets like it is totally normal. But it *isn't* totally normal. I write in my note-book: IS JIMMY PORKRINDS A SECRET SCHOLAR? A COAL BUFF FASCINATED BY THE HISTORY OF EARLY MINE LIFE? Let's find out, shall we?

The second weird thing that happens is this: Chuck Escapone licks a rat. They have these stuffed rats on barrels as you walk into the visitors center that very much remind me of Derrick Jonker. Escapone makes a big show out of licking one on the nose. Why? Why, newly popular psycho, why? A placard explains the purpose of the rats:

OH, RATS!

You are probably not too happy to see these creepy critters, but they were actually a welcome sight for miners. Miners believed that an absence of rats was a bad omen, a sign that an accident was about to occur. Turns out that there might have been some truth to this old mine tale. Scientists now theorize that the rats were sensitive to movements in the rocks that miners could not feel. If they were fleeing, it would be a good idea to follow them before the roof caved in!

Devon stands next to me reading the sign. He gives me a commiserating look, as if to apologize for the cave-in. I want to say, "It's OK, Dev. You didn't cause Dummy Halpin's death." Is he going to give me a hug? Zoinks. I step back, acting suddenly really interested in the tour guide who has emerged to lead our group.

"Miner Carl" is dressed in real period garb, with old-timey overalls, a miner's lantern helmet, and coal grime on his face. He shows us to a bin so we can each take a piece of coal for ourselves. The girls don't like that it messes up their hands. There is a nervous energy in the room. It is clear that *something* is going to happen, and everybody is waiting for "the moment."

Carl hands out miner helmets for everyone and then starts his speech.

"The history of coal mining is interesting and enlightening," he says, looking like he might weep from boredom. Is that a pun? En-*light*-ening because coal powers lamps? Is this going to be one of those tour guides who try to be funny? Then M.C. turns his back to me and speaks the rest of the tour into a little microphone. I am left, as it were, in the dark. My mind wanders, thinking about how Leigha looks beautiful even in a coal miner hat and Pat's too-big jacket. Would she be hot dressed as a nun? A lunch lady? A crossing guard?

This diverting train of thought is interrupted when I suddenly feel about seventy eyes turning on me at once. Despite the cool chill in the subterranean air, I am flushed. Then Pat Chambers raises his hand and says something like, "Excuse me, Miner Carl. I didn't realize ghosts could be, like, weird fat kids."

What the hell did I miss? Why can't ghosts be fat? And why is everybody . . . Oh crap. Miner Carl must've said something about the ghost of William Halpin, prompting Pat's brilliant comment. Leigha sort of covers her mouth like she knows she isn't supposed to laugh at the poor deaf kid. It is obvious that the highlight of this trip, the thing everyone will talk about afterward, is how funny Pat is, how ballsy and awesome it was that he actually raised his hand and made that crack about Halpin to Miner Freaking Carl. Hilarious!

With Arterberry's help, Miner Carl regains order and leads us to what literally is the end of the line. The path dead-ends where a wall of rock forms a cavernous room. Here stands a boulder so thick that even dynamite was useless. It is the spot where, all those years ago, the coal company couldn't go any farther in. They decided the only way to go was down, blasting precipitously into the nether reaches of the now-abandoned shaft. It is off-limits these days, carefully roped off, deemed way too dangerous. I see Pat leave his buddy on the other side of the room so he can teeter close to the edge with a smirk and pretend to lose his footing. Leigha has a weird look on her face as she watches him across the crowd. Panic? Fear that her ex might hurt himself? Why does she still care? C'mon, Leigha, there are other dudes, other options.

I lose her in the milling crowd.

A sick grin cracks the fake grime on M.C.'s face as he turns off the light on his helmet and introduces the finale. "Now it is the (*something something something*) to please shut your lanterns off on the count of three. I'll keep the light (*something something*)—just one minute will feel like an eternity. Imagine what it was like for these men every day of their lives (*blah blah blah*). Your eyes play tricks with you down here." I shut my light off early in case I can't pick up his count. I don't want to be the only one standing stupidly with mine on. A. J. Fischels does the same. . . . Hmm. Devon fiddles with his camera, then signals to me that he is going to climb one of the boulders jutting out of the side so he can get a good angle for his photo *of total darkness*. The rest of the class spreads with their buddies to the corners of the large, spooky room, milling around in excited anticipation.

"It will be the darkest thing you have ever seen or ever will see," Miner Carl declares.

Poof. There is a flash from Devon's camera and then total blackness. A chunk of time gone, like coal ripped from the earth.

The lack of light immediately lowers the temperature. When the lights come back on, I am shivering under my sweater and gloves but feeling charged up. Even though the trip has not been good for me, the experience of standing in the dark was actually exciting. I am realizing that light itself is a gift, that I am lucky to live where I live, when I do. What hell those miners lived through. Everything looks different after seeing nothing at all. I think I can see this realization in the gaze of some of my classmates—even Travis Bickerstokes seems subdued, looking around in squinty brightness, whispering about the lack-of-light show.

Miner Carl lets us soak it in for a few moments, then leads us back to the top of the path, where a strategically placed gift shop beckons. Most of the souvenirs are tacky pieces of crap like I SAW THE DARK T-shirts and pieces of coal labeled FUTURE

DIAMOND. Since they already gave us those magnificent lumps at the beginning of the trip, why would anyone spend money on something like that?

Devon buys two.

After we pay for our stuff, Arterberry and Prefontaine gather us up for the bus. We say a deeply heartfelt "Thank you, Miner Carl," and start to line up in the parking lot. The mood seems calm, maybe quieted by the cool and the dark. The weather is cooperating too. The sun ducks behind long bars of cloud, effectively letterboxing the sky. A bipolar breeze alternately whips us with frozen northern air and then suddenly turns as soft and warm as a kitten.

"Does everyone have their buddy (*something something something*)?" Miss Prefontaine is asking. Yes, Devon Smiley is standing so close that he's basically in my hip pocket. He is smiling and wearing his I SAW THE DARK mesh trucker hat. But it seems that two half sets of buddies are missing. Purple Phimmul indicates that Leigha Pennington is AWOL, and Derrick Jonker issues a similar report about Pat Chambers.

Devon nudges me with a suggestive elbow and wiggles his eyebrows beneath his dumb hat. I pick up on whispers, giggles, oohs and aahs. Planders blurts out, "No sex on game day!" Yeah, Planders, they are totally off doing it in the bottom of the mine. I had been hoping that the school's most famous on-again, off-again romance would remain off forever. Did Pat reseduce Leigha in the thrilling darkness? Jimmy Porkrinds—who knows why?—is grinning like a happy pumpkin. Even Chuck Escapone nods his hairy head as if in silent agreement with the crowd. This is *news*.

Prefontaine crosses her arms sharply and hangs her head like a toddler in time-out. Hmm . . . Then her eyes light up, and she points "There!" She actually signs it (although not on purpose—the real sign for "there" is just pointing at something). Indeed, Leigha is coming around the corner from the back of the gift shop. A sort of pale green and shifty embarrassment masks her face, and also . . . What is it? Her lipstick—when did she start wearing so much makeup?—is smeared.

"Where were you, young lady?" Prefontaine snaps. "We are all (*something something something*), and you've been, been . . ."

Apparently, she can't guess what Leigha had been doing. But I can. I am pretty sure it doesn't involve Pat Chambers. That look on her face is the look I had when I ate too much ice cream or, once, a whole bag of Baker's chocolate. The same look I had that day the cafeteria served fried ravioli.

Lovely Leigha's guts are in a full-on twist.

I want to shield my Leigha from the bad math whore. But I can't. So I just stand by, watching.

Leigha whispers to Miss Prefontaine. Prefontaine looks a little smirky, then gestures that Leigha should get in the back of the line.

The balloon of salacious excitement is popped. We turn to get on the bus—but where is Pat Chambers?

CHAPTER TWENTY-SIX

The next weird thing that happens: Miner Carl comes flying out of the Happy Memory Coal Mine emergency exit, screaming maniacally, a hyperball of panic. I can't tell what he is yelling, but it must be something like "Call the police" or "Dial 911" because dozens of people begin tapping their cell phones.

Devon, one of the many trying to get his cell phone to work, grabs me by the shoulders and explains with a look of serious concentration on his face.

"P-A-T I-S A-T T-H-E B-O-T-T-O-M O-F T-H-E M-I-N-E," he signs with shaking hands. "M-I-N-E-R C-A-R-L T-H-I-N-K-S H-E M-I-G-H-T B-E D-E-A-D."

For a lip-reader like me, a real emergency is quite literally like losing my mind. I catch fragmented bits of conversations, everyone on the cell phone at once, everyone panicking and running as if a sudden tornado of acid rain has opened over our heads. It is a madhouse. The Happy Memory employees—only used to pretending to work at a mine—turn to their leader, a panic-stricken bald man who just keeps running in circles yelling, "Ohmigod, ohmigod, ohmigod."

Miss Prefontaine has collapsed like a punctured implant, becoming a weeping puddle of makeup and tears, still clutching her oversize playing card. Mr. Arterberry is a dead ringer for a fish out of water, his big mouth gasping, his wide eyes staring in every direction.

A whirlwind of emergency vehicles whips into the parking lot—police cars, ambulances, and even fire trucks from several townships. Shouting into their shoulders, the EMTs run like a descending army into the mouth of the mine. I stand baffled and bathed in the colored strobe of the revolving lights. People next to me are hugging one another, crying. I feel dizzy.

Next: platoons of reporters, TV vans, even a helicopter, descend in a blink of an eye, like rats sniffing out a meal. They jab cameras and microphones in all directions, training their zoom lenses on tearstained faces. What should I do if they ask me for an interview? If they stick their cameras in *my* face? I decide that I will give them the finger. Solves the language issue and also makes my point. I hate it when newspeople ask someone how it feels when something tragic happens. How do they think it feels?

When the first wave of EMTs emerges from the mouth of the mine, I can tell that the news is grim. Though their faces wear masks of seen-it-all tough guys, the shock is clear in every one of their twitching eyes. Finally, like the exclamation point at the end of the sentence, the last group of workers emerges carrying a body bag. Pat Chambers is dead!

Fancy SUVs and Jaguars and pickup trucks cruise into the Happy Memory parking lot. Is it on the news already? No, of course: all those cell phone calls to Ma and Pa. Mom does have an old pager and always tells me to call "if there is ever any problem ever." I didn't even think to call.

I start to panic, because now how am I going to get home? Is Porkrinds driving us back to school? Do we have afternoon classes? What the hell is going on? I turn to Devon, who is looking in the other direction, toward the police cars. I can tell that he has recognized one of them. Duh . . . It is Mr. Smiley. Devon walks toward him.

Smiley Senior is not what I expect. Seeing him next to Devon makes me think not about genetics but about adoption. Bald except for a bushy mustache of epic proportions, he has a short, thick body and a face of sharp angles—the polar opposite of his son's features. It is clear that they are related, however, as he runs over and says to Devon, "Tell me what on earth is going on, my good man."

Devon fills Señor Smiley in on the details. Smiley the Elder nods quickly, like a dog trying to shake something off his head.

"Come on," he says, reaching up to throw an arm around Devon. "Let's get you out of this (*something something something*)."

Apparently, Devon has read my mind and said something to his father, because in a moment I am met by two somber Smileys gesturing toward the cruiser. They are offering me a ride home. I accept, feeling relieved. It is bizarre sliding into the back of a police car. I feel sort of important and tough. From fatass to badass. Mr. Smiley sits in the front with the officer who drove him there, a young guy who seems annoyed that he has to play chauffeur.

Devon and I sit hunched in the cramped seat. A row of scabbed metal bars and a sheet of Plexiglas separate us from the Law. There are no handles on the inside (of course), and the smell is a mix of sweat and steel and criminality. I start to feel claustrophobic and fear a panic attack coming on, a hyperventilation spell that would be the perfect cap to this fabulous field trip.

I close my eyes tightly and try not to think of anything. A blank haze fills my mind, and then I feel the car swing to a soft stop. We are in my driveway. Had I told either Smiley where I live? As if emerging from a dream, or maybe stepping into one, I get out and thank Team Smiley for the ride with a nod and salute. They return the gesture.

"Why didn't you call?" Mom is standing in the foyer signing angrily, then waving her pager like a foil in a jousting match. "And why are the police bringing you home?" Dad must be confused too, but he simply stands next to her, eating a handful of something.

"That's Devon, a . . . guy from school," I explain. "His father works for the police. He brought us home."

"Is it true what they are saying on the news?" she signs. "A boy from your school is . . ." Either she has forgotten the sign for "dead" or just can't bring herself to form the word.

I flip my hands over, finishing her sentence. "Dead" is an

odd sign, because it's very morbid yet somehow it makes you look like you're dancing. Dance move completed, I head straight for the TV.

My field trip is headline news. The first person I recognize on the screen is Marie Stepcoat, her eyes welling up at the memory of a guy who wouldn't bother to spit on her if she was on fire. Mrs. Stepcoat comes over and puts her arm around her daughter. Marie looks embarrassed at her mom's presence, like being cool is important even at such a moment.

Then the newscaster comes back on. The closed-captioner has to work fast to keep up with the breaking news. "Tragedy here in Carbon County. A teenage boy from Carbon High is dead after a ball at a lime." Poor Pat, victim of a citrus-themed dance? An imperfect art form, closed-captioning. It has been a Halpin family joke from happier times to laugh at weird captioning goof-ups on live TV. Once, the captioning for a live broadcast of an evacuation said people were "ejaculating from their homes." We go back to staring at the screen. The next person to show up on the screen is, to my surprise, Chuck Escapone. His normally sleepy eyes are fully alive, darting manically around like flies. "Sad day for everyone. . . . Big P will be missed. . . . Sad day."

Then, a split second before they cut to commercial, Jimmy Porkrinds leans into the frame, his head popping over Purple Phimmul's shaking shoulder. He grins. And then he blows the camera a kiss. Nutcase.

CHAPTER TWENTY-SEVEN

It is very early. The gloom of night hangs like a curtain over the town. I am vaguely, inexplicably, afraid. In the dazed instant between sleep and wakefulness, I feel I truly know what it is like to die. For Pat there will never be any of this. No more mornings. No more nights. High school is supposed to be something we all look back on and laugh about. Or maybe we look back and cringe. But we are supposed to look back—that much I get. It's not supposed to be all there is. . . .

Poof. He's gone.

Trying to chase the ghosts from my brain, I trudge to the kitchen to stuff my stomach. There is a bowl of chicken wings in the fridge. I eat every bit and then proceed to lick the bottom of the bowl. This doesn't make me feel better, so I fire up the computer.

Hello, world.

Online, the story has spread like a virus, reaching around the entire world. CNN, already interested in all things Chambers, gives Pat's death third-highest billing. Among all the events on the whole planet, only a nuclear scare somewhere and a massive bloody train crash in India rank as more important.

Principal Kroener, who I suddenly feel very bad for, is quoted a hundred million times with the same line. "We will look into this very seriously," he says.

Searching for more information, I find that TheTruthIsNot .com, a popular conspiracy page, has an article on the story. I had spent some time on their message board a while back, arguing passionately that the site itself is a government-run conspiracy. Man, did that get people mad. What TheTruthIsNot has to say this morning is this:

Another Republican Cover-up?

We are not heartless here at TheTruthIsNot. We are saddened whenever tragedy strikes, be it a village burned in Iraq or a death on a school field trip. We do not wish to make light of the death of Carbon High School student Patrick Chambers Jr. on his class trip to the (unfortunately named) Happy Memory Coal Mine.

We do, however, know the malodorous stench of foul play when we smell it.

Rumors are flying around Washington this morning that Pat Chambers Sr., the businessman under heavy fire for his involvement in the Laufman scandal, was about to reveal more information in the casino bribery and cover-up scheme. What kind of information? What did he know? What would people do to stop him? How high does this thing go? Can anybody say CIA hit man? POTUS?

Suddenly the light in the hallway flickers, and that weird sense of fear comes rushing back. I whip my head around like an attack dog staring down an intruder. It is just Mom. Of course.

"Time to get ready for school," she signs, tapping her watch. "Getting late."

I quickly shower, dress, and give Ace a few pats. My books seem pointless as I toss them into my bag. Who cares about any of this stuff? How can the world keep spinning no matter who falls off?

CHAPTER TWENTY-EIGHT

As I walk through the halls, I see half-teary whispered conversations. Several phrases are repeated, mostly "messed up" and "I can't believe it." There are other words too. Words like "suspicious" and "pushed." But I don't see anyone mouth the conspiracy theorist's favorite acronym. The only initials I see are *A.* and *J.* Everyone knows Fischels was furious about getting humiliated and uninvited. Is he responsible for Pat's death?

Arterberry announces that "we (*something something*) very special visitors today." He starts sending people one by one down to Principal Kroener's office.

When my turn comes, Arterberry waves in the overly showy way he always uses to communicate with me. Note to all: being deaf doesn't usually make one blind. As I head toward the door, Arterberry smiles encouragingly at me, and for a brief second, I see that he, like me, like the rest of us, is truly rattled by what happened. I realize—just for one second—that he is only a guy doing the best he can. I smile back at him, and he pats me on the shoulder.

A detective from the county boys in blue has taken over

Kroener's office. He's a large man with a tiny black notebook and a very official look about him. A no-nonsense police mustache is apparently standard issue along with the badge and gun. A Carbon High School tie tack is pressed into his sleek black tie. A former student? An alumni booster club member of our historically mediocre football team?

Kroener is there too, looking awkward on a folding chair under a surveillance camera that was, rumor had it, installed to protect students from his famous temper. Used to being the big dog, he is now relegated to the corner like a secretary.

Another person is there too. A lady cop. Mmm, sexy. Very young and very blond. She stands next to Hulk Mustache Man—a natural beauty in this unnatural setting.

"I'm Detective Hawley," he says to me. The interpreter signs it like she's not even there. Just like it's supposed to happen. Some people talk directly to the terp and talk around the deaf person in front of them, which is like the most annoying thing in the world. But I'm so stunned to see this beautiful interpreter in front of me that I do something bold. I hold up my index finger to Hawley—why do I already know that name?—indicating that he should give me a minute. I address the interpreter. But then I feel a little less bold.

If you've ever wondered if a deaf person can stutter in sign language, well, we can. I'm normally Mr. Fluent but get stuck on "I—I—I—I," until I blurt out, "I am pleased to meet you, my lady." My lady? Damn you, Devon Smiley! But she doesn't mind and instead signs her name—Melody—bestowing a luminescent smile upon me.

"I read lips pretty well, Melody," I sign. "You did not have to come all the way out here just for me."

"Would you like me to leave?" Melody asks, adding a little pout (with her lips, not her hands).

I am considering the possibility that she is flirting with me—a thought that is interrupted by Principal Kroener waving his hand and blurting out something like, "You guys going over signs like baseball players?"

"Something like that," she says. Then, signing to me: "Is he always like this?"

I nod my head yes and feel a warm glow. Yes, indeed, he is.

Kroener waves again and asks Melody, "Are you telling him to steal third base?" He thinks this is hilarious.

Melody and I simultaneously make the sign for "bastard" and crack each other up with swirling fingers. I am pretty sure no one else understands, but the men look disconcerted. Melody composes herself quickly, smoothing her crisp white blouse and resuming her "all-business" face—except for a tiny wink.

A wink! She *is* flirting with me. Unbelievable! Then the official questions start coming fast. What do I remember from that day? When was the last time I saw Patrick Chambers alive? Did I see anyone unusual hanging around our class? Melody and I don't get to flirt anymore, although we do share a subtle eyebrow raise when Detective Hawley asks if I saw *or heard* anything, anything at all, that was unusual.

His final question comes with a little preamble about how they don't suspect anyone from class and they don't want us to start getting suspicious of our classmates, but . . . who was my buddy, and can I account for his presence?

I sign to Melody that my buddy was Devon Smiley.

"Smiley?" she asks. "There is another Smiley?"

I nod and break into a totally over-the-top smile, crossing my eyes for effect.

She laughs blatantly at this and then offers a quick apology to Detective Hawley and Principal Kroener.

I don't want to admit that I was separated from Devon, so I say, "We were together most of the time."

"What time was this?" she asks.

The return question "What time do you get off work?" comes into my head, but I don't say it. I try to remember what stuff happened and answer as best I can, feeling my blood run cold. I don't exactly say that I was with Devon the whole time, but I don't exactly say that I wasn't either.

"Thank you," she signs. "You've been very helpful." Detective Hawley shakes my hand with his giant mitt. And then Kroener shakes my hand too for some reason. I have to leave. But I don't want to, not just yet. I can't let her go. I sign—not real sign language, just the sort of offhand sign language that everybody knows—to Detective Hawley that I would like him to tear a piece of paper out of his notebook and let me borrow his pen. He probably thinks I want to draw a map or something. I write my e-mail address down and fold the paper. I am so nervous that I fumble it and almost knock Melody over as I hand it to her on my way out. Smooth. I don't look back to see her reaction and am glad I won't know if anyone is laughing at me.

CHAPTER TWENTY-NINE

Ah, the weekend. Sleeping in late, avoiding the world, catching up on rest denied me by the inhuman hours of high school. Eating a box or two of doughnuts. The deep-fried pleasures that Saturday morning is intended for. I am denied all of these delights when Mom flicks on the lights at 9:30 a.m. Is she insane?

"You have a friend to see you," she says. I haven't talked to my friends lately. Who would visit me out here? I look confused. Mom smiles a huge smile.

"Why are you so happy?" I ask. But then I realize she is not smiling out of glee but is improvising a sign.

I scramble around my messy room for some clothes, settling on a particularly attractive pair of tan sweatpants and a Philadelphia Phillies shirt practically free of stains. I come up the basement steps to see Devon Smiley looking thrilled about something, rocking back and forth on his toes in the foyer.

Mom says something like "I'll let you two (*something something something*) carry on." Thanks, Mom. So how is this going to work? Then he hands me a small, slick black object. A Crony. Why is Devon giving me his favorite gadget? Then he reaches into his pocket and takes out another. He gestures that I should open it. I do, and he immediately starts texting. A message pops up on my screen.

> I remembered you had envied mine. Here you go, my good fellow!

I am truly stunned. Devon continues before I have a chance to answer.

> They can go online too! We can do IM rather than texting all the time, which does get expensive. We don't know who's getting the bill for yours, but I have to pay for mine!

It feels really weird, standing there in the foyer with the early-morning sun warming the cool air. I am having a conversation with my public school friend. It feels really normal, and pretty darn good.

After a minute of figuring out how to maneuver my fat fingers around the tiny keys, I deftly log on to my IM account. Devon follows me into the kitchen and sits down. We have milk. I chow on fistfuls of cereal straight out of the box. We're chatting!

HamburgerHalpin: u really didn't have to get this for me

Smiley_Man3ooo: It's my pleasure. Besides, it'll help with our investigation. With all the inside info I get from my dad and your big brain, we can solve this Chambers thing!

HamburgerHalpin: what r we--the freakin' hardy boys?

Smiley_Man3ooo: Yeah! I'll be Frank. I think he was the one with dark hair.

HamburgerHalpin: good. u b frank. now which one was the fat one?

Smiley_Man3ooo: I don't think either was fat. You stay pretty fit searching for hidden gold and climbing Skull Mountain and all that.

HamburgerHalpin: well which one was mad at everybody all the time?

Smiley_Man3ooo: The Hardys were always good-natured, optimistic, and charming lads.

HamburgerHalpin: i knew there was a reason i hated them

Smiley_Man3ooo: Oh, wait! I just remembered: they did have a husky friend named Chet! He was always eating Aunt Gertrude's cooking.

HamburgerHalpin: u r a giant dork

Smiley_Man3ooo: What the hell was his last name . . . ? It'll come 2 me. . . .

I notice that Devon Smiley is cursing more and using overly correct grammar less. I take pride in this. But the Hardy Boys? Who reads detective books from the thirties? I mean, besides me. He continues.

Smiley_Man3ooo: Got it. Chet Morton! He was, like, football-player fat, but still. It's a pretty good code name. You can be Chet, and I'll be Frank.

HamburgerHalpin: u didn't actually remember that. u opened a search while we were talking. that thing must have a browser

I feel a slightly awkward pause pass between us.

HamburgerHalpin: see--i'm already a hell of a private dick

I look up to see Devon's smiling face and crack a smile of my own. Then he turns serious.

Smiley_Man3ooo: It is really sad what happened to Pat.

HamburgerHalpin: yeah

Smiley_Man3ooo: Who do you think it was? Do you think it was someone who was mad about not getting invited to the party? A.J.? Do you want to help me find out?

HamburgerHalpin: why? u hated pat right? he flushed your suit

Smiley_Man3ooo: Smileys have been cops for three generations. Solving crimes is in my blood. Plus, I spent my childhood wearing out those Hardy Boys books from the library. I think I can take a crack at it!

HamburgerHalpin: aunt gertrude's cookin' better be good

Smiley_Man3ooo: So does that mean you are in?

HamburgerHalpin: let's do this frank

Smiley_Man3ooo: Great! Maybe if we figure this out, I can tell my dad what we've uncovered, and then he can get his promotion back.

HamburgerHalpin: howz that?

Smiley_Man3ooo: He got bumped down when they decided to promote some idiot yes men. They have him cataloging evidence. And you should see the way the old guy left the evidence room! It's a mess!

By the way, don't ask where that Crony came from. It would've just sat in a box for years anyway. ;)

HamburgerHalpin: hey thanks again for "lending" it. 2 me

Smiley_Man3ooo: I got myself a gift too: an ancient pistol that probably was used in some crime in 1930. Pretty sure it still works! But, yeah, glad to be of service, my good man.

HamburgerHalpin: dude stop with the devon-speak. it gets stuck in my head! i called a hot chick "my lady" yesterday

Smiley_Man3ooo: What?!?

HamburgerHalpin: did u see that blonde in kroener's office?

Smiley_Man3ooo: Yes. I assumed she was a newish detective? Or a student from the academy or something?

HamburgerHalpin: she was a sign language cop chick. she was there just for me

Smiley_Man3ooo: Lucky you.

HamburgerHalpin: i know right? and she was real flirty with me

Smiley_Man3ooo: No way!

I tell Devon all about Melody. I could keep chatting for hours. But then Devon reaches for his phone. He looks nervous again.

Smiley_Man3ooo: That was my dad. I didn't realize what time it is. We're going to go visit my grandfather. I'll come back later if that's OK.

HamburgerHalpin: ask him what other corny phrases might turn on a hot blonde

Smiley_Man3ooo: He lives in a retirement village on the other side of the mountain, so I don't know if he's into hot blondes, but maybe he could help you snare a sexy white-haired lady, which, if I remember correctly, is a type you love.

HamburgerHalpin: it is u who loves saggy boobs!!!

Smiley_Man3ooo: Hey, man, enjoy the Crony.

HamburgerHalpin: thnx again

Smiley_Man3ooo: Just don't get addicted.

CHAPTER THIRTY

I am totally addicted to my Crony. As soon as Devon comes back to my house, I gesture with it, hoping he will turn his on. Instead, he motions that I should hand him a pen and paper. He looks pale.

"I shouldn't have mentioned the evidence box in our chat," he writes. "I don't want anyone to know where we got the Crony." He is obviously nervous. His normally neat penmanship is very shaky. "Hawley would love to catch me and hold it against my dad."

"That's cool," I write. "Let's talk about other stuff. We'll never mention that again. Just fire up the Crony."

"Addict already?" he writes. I smile. "I really think it was someone who didn't get a playing card who committed the crime," he writes back.

"I guess our first question should be, Are we sure it was a crime?" I write. "Weren't they saying he might've just fallen?"

"That's what I wanted to tell you! My grandfather was talking about it. He used to be a cop too and has been kept in the loop. And my dad brings him case files."

Devon's penmanship has returned to its fine form. I am tired of writing, however. So I scribble: "I thought we were going to switch over to the Crony."

"Go ahead."

HamburgerHalpin: u were sayin'?

Smiley_Man3ooo: My grandfather's been following the Chambers case. He's constantly online.

HamburgerHalpin: he's not into those conspiracies like thetruthisnot.com is he?

Smiley_Man3ooo: What's that?

HamburgerHalpin: it's a crazy conspiracy site. they post stuff like ideas about how karl rove blew up the world trade center

Smiley_Man3ooo: What's their take on the Chambers case?!

HamburgerHalpin: they think pat was killed by a cia hit man to convince mr. c not to divulge any more information about the whole casino bribery thing. they believe this goes all the way to the president

Smiley_Man3ooo: So you like this site?

HamburgerHalpin: no they r nuts

Smiley_Man3ooo: How come you were on there, then?

HamburgerHalpin: oh it came up when i did a search for alternative news stories about the chambers case

Smiley_Man3ooo: Nice! I bet your computer skills will prove to be a crucial tool in our investigation. My dad and grandfather think that it really was a murder. The CSI types did some calculations on the angle that he landed, and they think he was pushed.

HamburgerHalpin: whoa. u r a crucial tool too

Smiley_Man3ooo: Plus, they found coal dust in his hair.

HamburgerHalpin: so?

Smiley_Man3ooo: My grandfather thinks that whoever pushed him whacked him on the head with a piece of coal--it would've knocked him out immediately. That's why no one heard him scream or anything.

HamburgerHalpin: i have wondered why i didn't hear anything

Smiley_Man3ooo: Funny! So, listen . . . Oh, wait, you can't.

HamburgerHalpin: *not* funny

Smiley_Man3ooo: Sorry! Couldn't resist. So, I told my dad and grandpa that everyone had access to coal: it was all over the place. But he said a buddy of his from the force told him they recovered the murder weapon. It had no fingerprints on it, which was weird, but they learned that it was bituminous, not anthracite.

HamburgerHalpin: and?

Smiley_Man3ooo: Well, remember those "future diamonds"?

HamburgerHalpin: yeah talk about lame

Smiley_Man3ooo: I put mine in my memory box.

HamburgerHalpin: you would

Smiley_Man3ooo: Those are actually real pieces of coal, but since Happy Memory is no longer active, they have to fly the souvenir coal in.

HamburgerHalpin: so?

Smiley_Man3ooo: The "future diamonds" were flown in from an active mine in western PA where they mine, get this, bituminous coal--just like what was found in Pat's hair. So it had to

be someone who was on the tour who killed
him!

HamburgerHalpin: that doesn't help narrow it down
too much

Smiley_Man3ooo: Probably it was someone from
our class!

HamburgerHalpin: maybe it was the ghost of
dummy halpin

Smiley_Man3ooo: Ha-ha.

HamburgerHalpin: u have any theories frank?

Smiley_Man3ooo: Well, Chet, if not a classmate,
maybe it was our bus driver. He came on the tour
too, didn't he? He always makes me feel a little . . .
unsettled.

HamburgerHalpin: who? jimmy porkrinds?

Oops! An unguarded moment. Devon looks up at me with
an odd smile on his face.

Smiley_Man3ooo: Did you say, "Jimmy Porkrinds"?

HamburgerHalpin: no, you must've misread

Smiley_Man3ooo: It's still on the screen.

HamburgerHalpin: it's just my little nickname for
him. you know no big whoop

Smiley_Man3ooo: And you say *I'm* weird.

HamburgerHalpin: u r weird

Smiley_Man3ooo: I guess so, but I rarely give nicknames to bus drivers based on snack foods.

HamburgerHalpin: rarely?

Smiley_Man3ooo: Well, once I did call my old bus driver Cupcake. But she was deliciously cute. Definitely wanted a taste of that frosting.

Smiley_Man3000 actually makes me laugh out loud.

HamburgerHalpin: you pervert. you love bus drivers. you have a total bus driver fetish

Smiley_Man3ooo: LOL. ROTFL.

HamburgerHalpin: LOL2BIFTLOLIS

Smiley_Man3ooo: What does that possibly mean, my good man?

HamburgerHalpin: laughing out loud too but I feel typing LOL is strange. i like making up acronyms

Smiley_Man3ooo: Fabulous. So, think we should check out this Jimmy Porkrinds? I can probably find his real name and address if I get my dad to tap into the school's files.

HamburgerHalpin: i don't know. u don't really think

he could be involved do u? what would his motive be?

Smiley_Man3ooo: Only one way to find out. Tomorrow we check out J.P. the BD. (That's "Jimmy Porkrinds the bus driver.")

HamburgerHalpin: i got that

Smiley_Man3ooo: Good night, Chet!

HamburgerHalpin: u have got 2 stop that . . . frank

I keep my Crony under my pillow, set to vibrate, in case Melody needs to contact me for "police business." Or if maybe my guerrilla toilet love letter inspires a desperate e-mail from one L.P. She might just need someone to talk with?

So when the Crony goes off at about midnight, my heart jumps a little bit. I leap up, check the screen, and see that it is not an e-mail but an instant message.

Smiley_Man3ooo: Hey, man, are you up?

HamburgerHalpin: i am now

Smiley_Man3ooo: Sorry to bother you.

HamburgerHalpin: it's all right. whaddya got?

Smiley_Man3ooo: I have a new theory.

HamburgerHalpin: is it that jimmy porkrinds is secretly a republican henchman hired to kill pat as revenge for pat senior ratting out the senator?

Smiley_Man3ooo: No, but that's good!

HamburgerHalpin: i was kidding

Smiley_Man3ooo: Oh.

HamburgerHalpin: so what's your theory?

Smiley_Man3ooo: Two words: Miss Prefontaine.

HamburgerHalpin: u think she killed pat?

Smiley_Man3ooo: There have been all these rumors that they were, you know, involved. Maybe that had something to do with it? To hide it? Because she was jealous?

HamburgerHalpin: omg. i just remembered something. a while ago i was looking at pat's web page. don't ask why

Smiley_Man3ooo: Why?

HamburgerHalpin: i said not to ask

Smiley_Man3ooo: Sorry.

HamburgerHalpin: there was a password-protected part called chambermaids

Smiley_Man3ooo: I wonder what that means.

HamburgerHalpin: r u kidding?

Smiley_Man3ooo: Yes. I'm kidding. I'm sure it was all about the ladies he's "loved."

HamburgerHalpin: right. so the little thing above it said "check out the newest addition" and addition was in italics

Smiley_Man3ooo: So?

HamburgerHalpin: so ADDITION

Smiley_Man3ooo: So?

HamburgerHalpin: don't you get it? what if that was like a pun because she's his math teacher!

Smiley_Man3ooo: OMG. You are a genius!

HamburgerHalpin: now we just have to hack into that password-protected part and c what we can c!

Smiley_Man3ooo: It was definitely risky when he called her Claire on the bus. And then you're saying that maybe she killed him to keep their secret from getting out?!

HamburgerHalpin: if you slept with pat chambers wouldn't you kill him to cover it up? her career would be trashed plus it's not like he was ever going to marry her right?

Smiley_Man3ooo: So, tomorrow I'll come over, we'll see what we can find on J.P., and then we can use your computer, if that's cool, to try to hack Pat's page.

HamburgerHalpin: cool with me daddy-o

I **wake up** very early the next morning. It is the second weekend morning I am up before noon—an unprecedented streak. I get dressed in a daze and go outside to wait for Devon. I am kicking stones in the driveway as he pulls up and parks his car, a beat-up former police cruiser, on my mom's flower bed. He does not seem to notice the damage to the mums. Instead, he hops out wearing a happy Hardy grin and clutching a file folder on which he has written "TOP SE-CRET" in big black letters. I roll my eyes. He laughs, waggles his eyebrows, and then hands me the folder. Inside is a typed note:

> Good morning, Chet! I trust you slept well. Sweet dreams of the fair Melody, perchance?
> You will be pleased to note that I have already located the address of one James Porkrinds. Our

quarry's name is actually Steven DiCielo—not as poetic as J.P., I agree. It seems that SDC, aka J.P., also drives a bus for my mom's school. She gave me his name, and I had my dad run a check on him. No criminal background, but I did get an address in an unusual location. He lives just one mile north of Happy Memory Coal Mine. Which raises an interesting question: Why would J.P. make a point of visiting the mine if he lives right around the corner? Wouldn't he have been there before? Perhaps he went on the tour because he was there to do some harm?

I look up and meet Devon's eyes so he knows I am finished reading. He looks at me expectantly, like he wants . . . something? I nod, even though it really doesn't seem to be the correct gesture. What am I agreeing with? Why would Porkrinds possibly want to kill Pat? Unless . . . Pat's death really was a warning to Pat Senior, and someone offered him a wad of cash, and . . . Probably not. But, then again, who knows? What are we going to do? Break into J.P.'s house? And what are we going to find that could possibly prove anything? A list taped to his mirror?

THINGS TO DO:

SHAVE (HEAD, NOT FACE).

CHOOSE PAIR OF SANDALS FOR MINE TRIP (MY FEET, MY BUSINESS).

DRIVE BUS TO COAL MINE.

CROSS THE PLOT, SMASH THE YELLOW LINE. JOKE
A MOLE, SMOKE A BOWL.

JOIN DUMB-ASS FIELD TRIP.

PUSH PAT CHAMBERS TO HIS DEATH AS PER
SECRET AGREEMENT WITH CIA.

MUWAA-HA-HA-HA-HA.

DEMAND MORE SANDALS FROM POTUS.

Is Devon just going to go up and knock on his door? Is this all Hardy hijinks to him? Are there fake mustaches and wigs in our future?

Devon takes a fake beard and dark glasses out of his backpack. I give him my most skeptical look. But when he snaps on the beard and glasses—voilà!—a perfect blind rabbi. I give him the universal look that says "Are you freaking serious?" He hands me a pair of glasses and my very own beard. I sign a very simple no. He shrugs and gestures for me to get in the car.

Driving to Happy Memory brings back disturbing feelings. The fact that Devon drives worse than a blind rabbi is also contributing to my shaky mood. It feels like so long ago that we took this same route. My mind goes fuzzy as I remember the scene: Pat handing out his cards, Mindy beaming, Escapone climbing over seats, A.J. looking fierce, and Miss Prefontaine blushing. It all seemed so important, and then, just as quickly, none of it matters at all. Death always seems like something that happens to someone else. I've never known it firsthand, except for toilet funerals for childhood fish. Thinking about how I cried back then makes me feel stupid when worse—so much worse—could be lurking around any corner.

As Devon points his cruiser up the mountain, we pass old miners' homes stained gray from years of coal dust. I see a strange little man sitting on a bench. Is he waiting for a bus? Or just waiting? For what? He has a shell-shocked look in his wrinkled eyes, and he seems as lost as anyone, as me, in this world. I think about what lies beneath the road we're on. Men died down there. We could be right on top of the spot where old Dummy himself took his last breath. I think of the pain he must have been in as his chest was crushed and his lungs filled with dust as black as death itself. I want to ask Devon to pull over so I can say a little prayer or whatever. But I just wait until we finally arrive at something called Gun Club Road and pull to the shoulder. Devon takes a deep breath and starts typing on his Crony.

Smiley_Man3ooo: 13 Gun Club Road is a few hundred yards ahead. The home of one Steven DiCielo.

HamburgerHalpin: what do we do now?

Smiley_Man3ooo: I was sort of hoping you'd figure out the plan from here. You're the brains.

HamburgerHalpin: i thought i was the looks and the muscle

Smiley_Man3ooo: You are the brawn. It's a subtle distinction but an important one.

HamburgerHalpin: what?

Smiley_Man3ooo: I don't know. Quit stalling. Make a plan.

HamburgerHalpin: what on earth r we doing here?

Smiley_Man3ooo: We're getting evidence to link J.P. to the crime.

HamburgerHalpin: devon please take off that beard. you look like an amish hippie

Smiley_Man3ooo: Ha-ha.

HamburgerHalpin: srsly what are we going to do?

Smiley_Man3ooo: Let's just see what we can see.

HamburgerHalpin: just go snoop around his house? u realize that he is a lunatic right? and maybe a murderer 4 hire? and he lives on gun club road. i'm not getting shot just so you can play real-life hardy boys

Smiley_Man3ooo: Don't be such a baby, Chet. And, besides, I happen to know that J.P. is not home.

HamburgerHalpin: how could you possibly know that?

Smiley_Man3ooo: My mom's class at the Catholic school has the Grammar Bowl this weekend. She said that Jimmy drives them every year. So we can go poke around his house with no fear of reprisal!

HamburgerHalpin: u think he just leaves his door open? and what would we possibly find anyway? i can't think of any non-nutty reason he would kill pat

Smiley_Man3ooo: Only one way to find out, my good man.

Devon yanks his beard back up and fixes it over his mouth like an old-timey robber readying his bandanna before a train heist. Then he snaps the glasses onto his face and checks himself out in the rearview mirror. And here's the thing: he does look sort of awesome. I pull out my own beard and glasses, put them on, and check the mirror. I look just like my dad. I furrow my brow and fold my arms, making Dad faces at myself.

Devon's reasoning behind parking the car a few hundred yards from Porkrinds's shady château is to "secure our cover," a move he probably learned in *The Hardy Boys in The Case of the Two Dorks Spying on Their Bus Driver.* This means a long walk up a steep hill to his house. My beard keeps tickling my nose. I'm sneezing, coughing, breathing heavily, and sweating buckets. My hair is a soggy mass of perspiration like I just got out of the pool.

I send Devon a message:

HamburgerHalpin: man i am a sweaty chet-y

Smiley_Man3ooo: Just think of it as sweating for truth and justice.

Up close, Porkrinds's house looks like a fortress. And, unless I am mistaken, all the windows are barred with homemade guards constructed of rebar. The front entrance is a heavy steel door, and the garage is protected by an intricate series of . . . booby traps?

Like a moat ringing a castle, a host of homemade alarms encircles the house. There are boxes balanced precariously on wooden sawhorses, strings rigged to door handles and windows, a blinking electronic eye. Devon looks at this crazy setup and then gapes back at me.

Smiley_Man3ooo: Whoa.

Is Porkrinds keeping a prisoner in there? Does he torture children who break the rules of bus etiquette? And then it hits me. Not only is there no way to get out of his garage, there is no way in. Unless . . .

HamburgerHalpin: frank i think we are onto something

Smiley_Man3ooo: I knew it! We have found the murderer! Why else would he come along on the trip? He must have done it! Now it's just a matter of motive and proof. I know you were joking, but I really think there might be something to the idea that he was hired by a political opponent of Pat's dad. You know, to silence him . . .

HamburgerHalpin: it has nothing to do with that

Smiley_Man3ooo: What? You said we were onto something.

HamburgerHalpin: drugs

But before I can further explain what I've figured out, Devon suddenly dives to the ground, pulling me with him. Then he forms his hand into the shape of a gun (coincidentally, the actual sign for "gun"). Someone is firing at us! I feel it too—the sound vibrations from the shots bouncing off my skin. He gestures that we should try to hide, as if I wasn't already thinking that. We scurry alongside the garage, the only place that offers any cover. This means knocking down dozens of the little booby traps, sending buckets and strings and nails flying everywhere. The red eye of the alarm blinks in double time.

Devon motions for me to lie flat on the ground. My whole life flashes before my eyes—sort of a sad show. I will make a better go of everything if I get out of here alive! Lose some pounds! Take a photography class! Sign up for yearbook! After staring up at the sky and making this pact with God, I look over at Devon. He is gesturing with his left hand that I should follow him. Then, with his right hand, he reaches into his belt and pulls out that old-timey pistol.

Devon points the barrel skyward and calmly squeezes the trigger. We start sprinting toward the car as he fires several more shots wildly into the air. In just a few seconds, I am down the hill, my feet kicking up dirt and gravel, my damn sunglasses sliding down my nose, beard flying into my eyes. Even though I can't hear anything and can hardly see, it is clear that imminent death is nipping at our heels, or butts.

Devon is much faster than I am, but he stays just a step ahead or so, running in a drunken zigzag pattern. I try to keep up, zigging when he zags. The strategy seems to be working—we are almost back at the car and are still not dead! After one final sprint, I am pawing at the car door handle. Devon strains to unlock the passenger side while aiming the gun with one hand, wildly scanning the sky for our would-be assassin. I dive into the car, and he jams the key in the ignition and peels away down Gun Club Road with a look on his reddened face that can only be described as . . . deranged happiness?

What the fudge!

CHAPTER THIRTY-THREE

We are back at my house. I am pacing like a maniac, trying to calm down. Ace paces along with me, and Devon seems more excited than ever.

"Don't you think we should have called the cops?" I write on my little pad.

"Didn't I tell you? They were already coming. I heard sirens. Somebody must have called them about the shooting."

"Holy crap! You think they will bust Porkrinds for drugs? I read his lips on the bus. He's mumbled stuff about smoking before, and about digging holes. There must be an underground entrance to his stash."

"I guess. But, well, I really wish we had solved the murder. Who cares if the bus driver is a pothead? They all are. It's a well-known fact."

"Even Cupcake?"

"An exceptional exception. But, hey, we still have another task: hacking Pat's ChamberMaids page."

"I think I have had enough for today," I write.

"Come on!" Devon writes. "We are getting close to something, I can feel it!"

"Devon, don't you even realize that someone was trying to *kill* us?"

"Oh, they were just trying to scare us off," Devon writes.

"Well, it worked. I'm scared and I'm off this."

"This is just peeking around online. And, besides, now we have this noble beast to protect us."

He has a point, though not about Ace. We probably aren't going to get shot in my computer room. Plus, I have a hunch that there might be something very interesting on that Chamber-Maids page.

"Come on," I write. "Upstairs." A gesture to Ace is all he needs to follow us.

Devon seems impressed by my computer. The Halpins, if you haven't noticed, aren't exactly rolling in dough, but a brother like me needs a nice PC. So I modified an old computer we got at a yard sale with a motherboard we bought used on eBay. I cobbled together some freeware and other (ahem) sort of freeware that I downloaded. Then I sort of stole the Internet connection from our neighbor's wireless and was good to go. It is a sweet setup, if I say so myself.

"You ready?" Devon writes.

"As I'll ever be," I write back.

We set about the task of hacking Pat's locked page. Truth

is, I've only ever hacked a few passwords: my dad's, which was easy ("KenDog," his dubious nickname for himself), and the one on the computer at my old school, which was, believe it or not, "password." To hack into Pat's, I do some quick math and try a few variations of his name and the year he was born. Nothing. Then I try a few words that, although officially banned by Principal Kroener's latest "language law," I had seen come off Pat's lips. Nothing, nothing, and nothing.

Again, the page locks itself, saying "sorry 4 u, suckah." Was Pat smarter than I gave him credit for? I pound both my fists into my forehead and slump over in a big mound. Ace nudges me sympathetically with his cold snout. Devon takes the exact opposite approach, suddenly leaping up all hyper and spazzy. He looks deep in thought for a moment, then taps a few buttons on the keyboard. The page slowly scrolls to life.

I make the face that universally means "How the crap did you do that?" And then I punch Devon in the arm. He does that weird eyebrow wiggle he always does. I punch him again.

"It was easy," he writes, elbowing me aside to get at the keyboard. He opens up the word processor and types: "You just have to know your subject."

"What do you know about Pat Chambers?" I type.

"I know that passwords often require a number along with a name. The name is, of course, his own, as Pat is totally in love with himself. Or was."

"That much I knew."

"Yeah, but you didn't think about what number would come to mind when someone like Pat had to think of a number."

He is right—I didn't.

"It's his football number!!!! Forty-five!"

"You would know that," I typed.

"I would and I did, and you're just jealous. To be a good forensic scientist, you have to know everything about everything in life, not just the things that you think are important."

"Tru, n u suck."

We had assumed Pat's ChamberMaids page was devoted to the ladies of his life.

It is.

Pictures and pictures and more pictures scroll up on the screen of various women in various degrees of undress. It seems as though Pat had taken them with either a cell phone camera or a hidden device somewhere in his room. The pictures are grainy and blurry. We can't see too many faces, but there is a blond ponytail I clearly recognize. Even in her compromising, uh, position, it is obvious who it is. Devon recognizes it too.

"I-S T-H-A-T M-I-N-D-Y S-P-A-R-K?" he signs. Of course. We high-five. I'm not sure at all why we do this.

The moment passes as we both recognize the prettiest girl in the world. Pat captured a picture of Leigha, mostly unclothed, on his bed. All her naughtiest bits are covered, but still I'm blushing and feeling a heart attack coming on. Pat is smirking cockily, while the look on her face is . . . hard to read. I haven't seen any girls in the throes of passion, but I'm pretty sure they don't look like this. Her eyes are vacant, and her mouth is tight and grim, like she's scared. Was she? Devon pats me on the back in a consoling way. Thanks? Does he notice what I see in her face? Is it really there, or am I just wishing?

Before this sinks in, Devon moves on to the next picture. There is a detail we can see very clearly beyond any doubt: a tattoo of a dolphin leaping out of the left cup of a lacy black bra. The bearer of that tattoo was in Pat Chambers's bedroom. The bearer of that tattoo was, shock and awe, Miss Prefontaine.

Devon and I stare at each other wildly. Our mouths open and close silently like a pair of dying trout. Neither of us can speak. Finally, I am able to sign three shaky letters. "O-M-G," I say to Devon.

Devon repeats, with a little embellishment: "O-M-F-G."

Thing is, we knew, or thought we knew, that's what we would find. But actually seeing it there is still a shock.

So, should we tell someone? I look at Devon and nod once, the sort of solemn greeting you'd give a fellow mourner at a funeral. Yes, we should.

What to do? Who to call? Shouldn't there be a pamphlet about this kind of thing like the ones they have in the nurse's office explaining menstruation and bipolar disorder? I picture those cartoon circle heads explaining teacher-student affairs. They should have a tip line like they have for guns in school or suicide. "Have evidence that your math teacher is showing her dolphin to one of your classmates? Call 1-800-EDU-SXXX." Hmm . . . While I'm lost in this thought, Devon taps me on the shoulder. He has fired up the Crony and is typing a question.

Smiley_Man3ooo: Thinking about a particular aquatic mammal?

HamburgerHalpin: u know it

A lie, but a harmless one.

Smiley_Man3ooo: So, should I tell my dad?

I nod, and he reaches for his phone. I type fast before he can dial.

HamburgerHalpin: wait! why don't we just e-mail the picture to the cops anonymously?

We chat about how this is going to be a huge scandal. There will be tons of questions, possibly lots of publicity, and if it gets back that Devon and I were the ones who ratted out Prefontaine . . . Well, let's just say that Pat wasn't the only one who enjoyed having The Dolphin around. Neither of us needs any more reasons for people to beat us up.

We decide to make a fake e-mail account with a sincere crime-stopper name (good_citizen2247@gmail.com) and set to composing a really cheesy message. We want it to seem like it was sent by an old person, so we use the computer's thesaurus to make our vocabulary ancient and formal. Old people love e-mail. Also, because I'm a total genius, I find a way to mask my IP address so no one can trace where our letter comes from.

Dear Police Department,

It has recently come to my awareness that a scholar at Carbon High has been drawn into a sex liaison with one of his educationalists. I deem that the female in this photograph is in fact the teacher known as Miss Prefontaine. It was taken from an infantile lad's Web page. Here is the link. Password: Chambers45. Attached is the picture. Do thee as thou wilt!

Sincerely yours,

Concerned Citizen

We sit back and admire our handiwork. There is no way anyone could guess that it was written by a high school student. But, still, I feel nervous. Even though we haven't really done anything felonious, we check and recheck a dozen times to make sure the incriminating JPG is really deleted from my computer. And now we wait for whatever comes next. How long will it be until Good_Citizen's actions set the trap that snares The Dolphin?

CHAPTER THIRTY-FOUR

Behold the pernicious reach of technopower. That very night the local TV news is flashing a slightly fuzzed-out picture of the dolphin tattoo and running a clip of Miss Prefontaine with her head hidden under a jacket on her way into the police station. I watch as they play that clip over and over and over again. It becomes the headline of the Sunday local news and even makes that little crawl at the bottom on the weather channel. From what I can figure (my grasp of the facts is hazy due to some epically bad closed-captioning), here's what happened:

Not long after we sent the e-mail, the cops went to Miss Prefontaine's house. They couldn't have gone in with the idea that they were going to arrest her from just an anonymous e-mail, right? So it must have been simply to question her about the picture and the message. However, apparently they found a "sick shrine" to Pat Chambers in her apartment. Miss

Prefontaine started acting hysterical, and the cops brought her to the police station. Somehow the local press got wind of it, and the cameras were there to film her arrival. Even with the stupid misspellings of the closed-captioning, I could figure out that she wasn't "fried" but rather undeniably fired.

The rabid newshounds are interviewing anyone they can find. Mr. Arterberry is on camera pretending to be shocked, although I am pretty sure he had to know about it. How could he not? Thinking about it now, how could anyone not have known? The cameras also find Planders somehow. His mouth hangs half open, and he says the word "uh" more than a dozen times in two sentences.

There are also some random students I barely recognize (who are these people?) saying clichéd things.

"She was always really nice."

"I'm really shocked."

"It's just not right. She was a good teacher. I learned so much."

This all sounds eerily familiar, like *she's* the new dead one.

The whole thing is so . . . savage. Was sending the e-mail the right thing to do? Did I have pure motives? Did Devon? Now all anyone wants to talk about is the teacher Pat was getting it on with.

I start to wonder: What were Pat's thoughts on this? Was nailing her something he felt like he had to do? Was his whole life just doing things he had to do?

And why do I keep finding myself thinking: Are we missing a clue? How did I get myself caught up in this mystery thingy anyway? Why do I even care? I can't answer that, even to myself. But I am in it. Deep.

CHAPTER THIRTY-FIVE

Later that night I feel the teasing vibrations of my Crony and jump up, thinking maybe it is Melody or Leigha, although that is as likely as my winning the Boston Marathon. Now, maybe if it was a Boston Cream Pie Marathon . . . mmmm.

Smiley_Man3ooo: Hey, Chet, you watch the news?!

HamburgerHalpin: sure did frank. can't believe how fast that happened

Smiley_Man3ooo: What do you think it all means?

HamburgerHalpin: i have no idea

Smiley_Man3ooo: First the shooting at J.P.'s house and his arrest and now this. It has to be related somehow.

HamburgerHalpin: wait! did you say jimmy porkrinds got arrested?

Smiley_Man3ooo: Yeah! Second story after Prefontaine! You were right. They found a ton of weed in that garage! And a secret tunnel!

HamburgerHalpin: holy crap!

Smiley_Man3ooo: Hey, did you see Planders on the news?

HamburgerHalpin: uh uh uh yeah uh uh uh

Smiley_Man3ooo: It all has to be related somehow. And it all has to be related to this murder.

HamburgerHalpin: i really don't think so frank. i think the thing at jp's just had to do with him wanting to protect his crop and the thing with prefontaine might mean something but i'm not sure what. maybe it's just a coincidence. and hey i never asked you: why wasn't jp at the grammar rodeo or whatever?

Smiley_Man3ooo: Oh yeah, I asked my mom. Turns out it is next weekend. Sorry about that.

HamburgerHalpin: apology not accepted. and what the hell were you doing with that gun?

Smiley_Man3ooo: It's a dangerous world out there, Chet. Life isn't really a Hardy Boys novel.

HamburgerHalpin: no but man it was a helluva day

Smiley_Man3ooo: You don't know the half of it.

HamburgerHalpin: what do you mean?

Smiley_Man3ooo: Something else happened.

HamburgerHalpin: a girl talked to you and you didn't run screaming from the room?

Smiley_Man3ooo: Hey, I've had girlfriends.

HamburgerHalpin: they all live in canada?

Smiley_Man3ooo: Same place yours live.

HamburgerHalpin: i had a girlfriend next county over. she went to my old school with me. her name was ebony and she was great. but who cares? what else happened today? don't keep the fat guy in suspense

Smiley_Man3ooo: My dad told me . . . Swear you won't tell anyone that I'm giving you confidential police information?

HamburgerHalpin: i swear on leigha pennington's sweet little tush

Smiley_Man3ooo: They have a crazy new suspect in Pat's case.

HamburgerHalpin: are they tied into the vast republican conspiracy?

Smiley_Man3ooo: No! It's you!

HamburgerHalpin: u r kidding

Smiley_Man3ooo: I told them they are way off.

HamburgerHalpin: waaaaaaaaaay off

Smiley_Man3ooo: I know! LOL. But I guess in one of the interviews with Detective Hawley, someone mentioned that crack Pat made about you that day, how he said something to Miner Carl about ghosts being fat.

HamburgerHalpin: thanks for reminding me

Smiley_Man3ooo: Yeah, well, I guess some genius thought maybe you were the one who did it then.

HamburgerHalpin: i see

Smiley_Man3ooo: But I told my dad they are barking up the wrong tree.

HamburgerHalpin: arf arf

Smiley_Man3ooo: I wouldn't worry too much. If there is nothing to the Prefontaine or Porkrinds angles, I still think the best bet is A. J. Fischels. That brings us to the next part of the plan.

HamburgerHalpin: do i seem worried?

Smiley_Man3ooo: I just mean--I didn't even tell you this--right after that thing with Hawley, they were looking at me as a suspect!

HamburgerHalpin: rly?

Smiley_Man3ooo: It is so dumb. I guess someone told them about how Pat used to bother me and stuff. As if someone would kill over that nonsense.

HamburgerHalpin: too absurd

Smiley_Man3ooo: I think Hawley just has it in for my 'dad and is trying to take it out on me.

HamburgerHalpin: prolly

Smiley_Man3ooo: Oh, and also they found a long black hair on Pat's body. They thought it was from my awesome ponytail.

HamburgerHalpin: you do shed like a nervous poodle. but why are they looking at me? i haven't had long hair since my unfortunate mullet in 4th grade

Smiley_Man3ooo: It turns out it was dog hair. At first they didn't realize.

HamburgerHalpin: did u tell them about ace?

Smiley_Man3ooo: Nah. I said, "He's deaf, not blind." Jerks! Saved you the trouble of having to deal with the cops again. Although maybe I should have let you have the chance to see your girlfriend Melody again.

HamburgerHalpin: damn u frank!

Smiley_Man3ooo: So, next part of the plan. We sneak into school tomorrow, check out the security camera footage of everyone being interviewed in Kroener's office. You'll read their lips, and we'll know what everyone said!

HamburgerHalpin: there won't be anything in those tapes the cops don't already know about

Smiley_Man3ooo: Yeah, but they don't know what we know. I bet we could get clues that they missed. I'm sure of it! It's flawless!

HamburgerHalpin: i can think of about 47 flaws and i'm not even trying that hard

Smiley_Man3ooo: Like what?

HamburgerHalpin: like the fact that your last flawless plan resulted in a hail of gunfire

Smiley_Man3ooo: A minor miscalculation.

HamburgerHalpin: and how are we going to get in? how do we even know how to use the equipment? and do you have any idea how many hours it would take to lip-read and transcribe all those tapes?

Smiley_Man3ooo: For the first two points, just relax and trust in the Smileyman. I swear, I have a great plan this time. And to speed up the process, well, that's easy: we bring backup.

HamburgerHalpin: what the hell do u mean?

Smiley_Man3ooo: You claim to have a certain

ex-girlfriend who is a fantastic lip-reader. Unless you were lying about her existence.

HamburgerHalpin: ebony is real! unlike your canadian "girlfriend" that you wish you had

Smiley_Man3ooo: If she's real, then let her know I'll pick her up in the Smileywagon tomorrow. The building will still be open for in-service teacher training.

HamburgerHalpin: i can't believe i'm doing this but fine i'll ask if she's up for it. i can't make any promises though

Smiley_Man3ooo: Awesome! Flawless!

HamburgerHalpin: stop saying that. and leave the pistol at home will ya?

I still have Ebony as a "buddy" even though we haven't chatted in a while. It didn't end badly or anything—it was just a growing apart based to some extent on a (possibly stupid) dispute that led to me leaving the school and her behind. It might not make any sense if you're not deaf. Allow me to explain anyway. Ebony is a lot like me. At first glance you might not think so, since she's black and really cute, and I'm, well, not. But we both grew up with "problems with our ears" but could hear somewhat for most of our early lives. (That's how come I can read lips and write so well.) But Ebony is sort of a political deaf person who agrees with a lot of "prelingually" deaf people.

These people usually have sign language as a first language and sometimes don't learn English at all. (And, yes, sign language is a totally different language from English, with its own grammar and everything. Technically, I'm bilingual, which is cool.) They also often have strong feelings about "deaf culture" and really like to harangue you in signed webcam diatribes if you are a postlingually deaf smart-ass who posts aberrant views on their message boards. I have a lot in common with them, like how I refuse to wear hearing aids and prefer sign language over speaking, but with me that's not part of some grand political stance.

So Ebony and I were joking once about having deaf babies, which was definitely a joke, since we didn't even get all the way to second base. (I guess you could say I got thrown out trying to stretch a single into a double?) I said something about how we'd have to look into the cochlear implant so our deaf baby could hear. Upon hearing this (hah), Ebony got seriously pissed. The cochlear implant is sometimes called the bionic ear, a device that is implanted in your head (or something, I'm not a surgeon) that lets deaf people hear. Any chance to be a bionic anything would be cool, but Ebony (and, to be fair, lots of deaf people) gets really mad about the idea that deafness is a disability and something you need to be cured of. People who are deaf should be damn proud of it, she said. More power to them, I said, but I'd want our baby to be able to hear if it was an option. This was so theoretical that I can't believe we had a fight about it, especially since the baby, *which didn't exist,* probably wouldn't be a candidate for the bionic ear anyway, since you have to have a certain type of deafness, which neither Ebony nor I do.

So she got pissed, and we never got to make babies or even round another base. And then we broke up. And maybe we weren't really "boyfriend and girlfriend" to begin with. We just chatted online a lot, goofed on everyone together, and awkwardly made out once in a shed.

Devon's plan won't work without another lip-reader. And Ebony is ridiculously good. She is the one who should have been in mainstream ed at CHS. But maybe she doesn't care what other people think. And maybe she is onto something. Who wants to be normal anyway?

I check my buddy list and see that she is indeed online. Deaf people seriously love themselves some Internet.

HamburgerHalpin: what's up you cretin?

Def4Life: omg, heapin' halpin! i was just thinking about u!

HamburgerHalpin: i do have that effect on the ladies. i'm the hottest deaf guy since lou ferrigno

Def4Life: don't flatter yourself--have u ever checked out how fine his ass was?

HamburgerHalpin: can't say that i have

Def4Life: well, u definitely should. the hulk wore those torn little pants. damn!

HamburgerHalpin: shockingly i never noticed

Def4Life: i could talk about lou ferrigno's ass all

day, but that's probably not why you messaged me. so what is up?

HamburgerHalpin: first why don't u tell me why u were thinking about me?

Def4Life: since the other day--i was wondering if u were on that field trip where that public school kid died. u know--after u abandoned me.

HamburgerHalpin: yeah. that's actually sort of why i wanted to talk to u

Def4Life: ?

HamburgerHalpin: i have this friend . . . he thinks we can solve the case

Def4Life: didn't the kid just fall or whatever?

HamburgerHalpin: we r pretty sure he was pushed

Def4Life: !

HamburgerHalpin: yeah so my friend thinks we can figure out who did it if we break into the school and lip-read some surveillance tapes of cops interviewing the people at chs

Def4Life: and you need some blackup?

HamburgerHalpin: don't u mean backup?

Def4Life: i stand by what i said.

HamburgerHalpin: so ummm yeah we could use

your skills. your school is closed tomorrow for teacher in-service too right?

Def4Life: soooo, u come calling to the lip-reading champion. u admit that i'm better!

HamburgerHalpin: don't flatter yourself. there's just a lot of tapes and my friend thinks the only way we can get through them all is if--

Def4Life: i'll do it.

HamburgerHalpin: wait what? u will?

Def4Life: sure! how exciting! it'll be just like living out a nancy drew novel.

HamburgerHalpin: oh man u have got 2 b kidding me

Def4Life: what? i loved those books when i was little. what's wrong with nancy drew? a lot of perfectly intelligent people like nancy drew!! even if she was a little racist . . .

HamburgerHalpin: sheesh. don't wet yourself ebony. it's just that this friend of mine devon smiley--he's obsessed with the hardy boys.

Def4Life: it's a real mystery! let's go sleuthing!

HamburgerHalpin: yeah whatever. so we'll pick you up real early tomorrow

Def4Life: i'm free in the morning, but i have karate in the afternoon.

HamburgerHalpin: why did u start taking karate?

Def4Life: to learn the best way to break the fingers of fat kids who try to stick their hands up my shirt. when did you get a car?

HamburgerHalpin: not mine. it's devon's

Def4Life: he's got a car and is into daring hardy boys style adventure? seems like ur friend devon smiley is someone i def want to meet. c ya tomorrow, will halpin!

HamburgerHalpin: he's not quite as cool as all that but yeah we'll see ya at like 7 in the morning

I write back to Devon, who is already online too (he spends so much time on IM that, along with his skills at signing, I am thinking about making him an honorary deafie), and tell him Ebony is up for the plan. I have a few questions about the rest of his scheme, but all he will say is "Trust the Smileyman."

I will go along with his plan. I have to. I want to see those tapes. I need to see those tapes.

Devon assures me that I don't have to worry about the investigation into their "crazy new suspect," but I feel the dance of nervous butterflies. I sit there thinking, breathing slowly, tapping on my keys, not really typing anything, just feeling the slick plastic beneath my fingers. Are we getting closer to the truth or further and further from it? Will I have to prove my own innocence?

CHAPTER THIRTY-SIX

Monday. We are off from school (one of those in-service days when teachers get paid for a day of work but just come to school to have a cocktail party in the teachers' lounge— possibly?), but I have to get up early. Crime solving is inconvenient. I tell Mom we are going to school to participate in a vigil for Pat, a thing that actually is happening, although much later in the day.

I wait outside on the still-dew-moistened lawn for Devon's beat-up former police car (aka the Smileywagon) to retrample Mom's flowers. My notebook is out, and I am flipping through, rereading the notes I have accumulated on Carbon High. I also have my fake beard with me and am pulling it on just as Devon careens into the driveway. As expected, he mashes the mums. He gets out and tries to fix the damage, rescuing a damaged stalk and putting it in his pocket. He makes a face to let me know he is sorry about that. Then he starts cracking up and gestures for the pad and pencil.

"What's up with the beard?" he writes. "This isn't an under-cover mission."

I write back, "Oh yeah, I knew that." Why *am* I wearing the beard? I shove it back in my pocket. Devon laughs. I force a weak grin. I had written out directions to Ebony's place on a page in my notebook and flip to it, showing Devon the way. I spend most of the drive badgering Devon by breathing on the window to steam it up and then writing "WHAT IS THE FREAKING PLAN???" over and over again. Devon, unfortunately, has learned the sign for "Trust me."

The Smileywagon pulls up to Ebony's house. She is standing out front waiting for us, basically bouncing on her toes with excitement. Devon looks at her and then me and then her. He mouths, "She's black." I palm my cheek and act shocked. Devon shrugs and Ebony jumps in the back, waving happily to the both of us. I blow her a kiss. Devon still seems a little flustered by her unexpected blackitude. (Wasn't the fact that her name is Ebony some sort of clue, Frank?) He obviously panics as he tries to remember the signs he had learned for the occasion. Then he signs, "Good morning! I am very happy to have us with you." Nice try, Dev.

Ebony signs back very politely, "Nice ride," even though it totally isn't. The car lurches into drive, and we are off. Ebony notices the note I had written on the window. She taps Devon on the shoulder and points to it. Devon repeats his mantra: "Trust me." Then he sideswipes a bush.

Since only teachers are in attendance, the school parking lot is sparsely populated. I can see that Ebony is confused by the fact that Devon parks at the extreme end of the lot near the soccer fields, past about a hundred closer spaces. I find myself thinking of Devon's words from the Porkrinds mission and trying to convey in signs that it is to "secure our cover." Oddly, Ebony actually seems to think this is a good idea. This must have been a maneuver in *Nancy Drew in The Fat, Black, and Smiley Mystery.*

My hope that Devon won't do anything too embarrassing is squashed when he unfolds two copies of a new top-secret file folder explaining the day's mission. He hands one to each of us. Ebony doesn't flinch, as if getting this file is totally normal. I read:

Good day, my coconspirators! Thank you for putting your trust in the Smileyman. I assure you, this time I have a solid plan. The school is unlocked so the teachers can come in for their meetings. And I know all about the surveillance system! Smiley Security Services is a sideline my father started. He and I actually installed the school's T1300 digital backup system. Getting what we need will be relatively easy, due to the auto time-stamping and the fact that we only need to pull from one camera (the one in Kroener's office) to find the footage from last Friday. I can dump half the footage to each of the two stations down in the janitor's office, and you can each read what was said to the police. Clues will abound! Good luck and Godspeed-reading!

Ebony gives a serious nod and then signs to me, "I like him already."

"Not so fast," I sign. And then, so Devon can see, I finger-spell, "H-O-W A-R-E W-E G-O-I-N-G T-O E-X-P-L-A-I-N W-H-A-T W-E A-R-E D-O-I-N-G T-H-E-R-E?"

Devon looks perplexed. My stomach lurches. He hadn't thought of this? What if we get caught? Our janitor, a kind, shriveled little man whose name tag indicates the curious moniker of Lucille, doesn't seem like the murderous type, but I am not trusting anyone anymore. Then Devon laughs and gives an informal sign indicating that I should flip over my paper. On the back it says:

Will, don't be all nervous about us getting caught. Janitors and all other support staff have the day off. I am 110% sure this time.

I look up and see him wiggling his eyebrows triumphantly. And I have to admit that the Smileyman has thought of pretty much everything. The three of us strut across the parking lot like the Odd Squad. Entering the school's main corridor, I feel exposed and nervous, but Devon quickly finds a door that leads to a back stairwell going down to the basement. It is just about as charming as you'd expect the basement of a public high school to be—and, as Devon had predicted, totally deserted. Still, to my nervous eye, danger lurks in every shadow.

I am about to open the door to the janitor's office when Devon grabs me and steps in front. He indicates that I should wait and points to the tips of his fingers, improvising a sign for fingerprints. He wears a handkerchief over his hand like a sock puppet while he flicks on the lights. The janitor's room is a nasty little rat cave with a multitude of gray stains of unknown origin all over. Devon quickly turns on the two monitors and begins both typing furiously and scrolling maniacally with the mouse while somehow keeping the handkerchief on any surface he is touching. He had indicated that he needed my computer skills to help solve the case, but he obviously knows more than he let on. Ebony also seems impressed. "He is good," she signs.

Devon searches for Friday's footage on the server while I fill Ebony in on the details. I let her know about the party, the field trip, and who our main suspects are.

"What are we looking for?" Ebony asks me.

"I guess we'll know it when we see it," I lamely respond. "Or if you are so good at lipreading, just write down everything everyone says." I go to rip out a page from my notebook. She smirks, shows me that she brought her own notebook (labeled TOP SECRET), and signs, "The game is afoot."

Devon has done it. Marie Stepcoat's nervous face appears on the monitor in front of me while the dopey grin of Chuck Escapone pops up on Ebony's screen. He gives the informal sign that we should get to it. He signs, "I'll keep watch," which he must have learned just for the occasion.

We scribble transcriptions like it's a race, quickly going through all the suspects. We see Marie Stepcoat and Chuck Escapone, Kevin Planders and Derrick Jonker. Suddenly I feel an elbow in my ribs. Ebony is laughing. She points to her screen. A huge rear end is waddling in front of the camera, taking up pretty much the whole picture.

"Christ," I sign. "Am I really such a wide load?" She nods. I redden a little and press fast-forward on her screen so we don't have to keep looking at my balloon face. Devon sticks his head in to see why Ebony is laughing. Ebony points and signs, "Big boy." Devon grins. And then we see his grin in double—he is on the screen right after me. Devon indicates that we should skip that interview. He grabs the keypad, making his interview fly by at double time. He looks like a mental patient, the way his nervous gestures are sped up like that. Why doesn't he want us to see what he had to say? Is he just saving time? Once his interview is over, he lets the footage play normally and goes back out to his guard post in the hallway.

My footage starts to run together, the same answers to the same questions. No one saw anything, no one left their buddy, no one knew nothing 'bout nothing. Ebony taps me on the shoulder. "I hate to admit that I am having trouble here," she signs. "But did that girl just say her name was *Purple*?" I look up and see Miss Phimmul's cocky sneer on Ebony's screen. I laugh. "Public school girls are strange birds," I sign. "Her name really is *Purple, Ebony*." Ebony shakes her head, apparently not noting the irony.

Then A. J. Fischels appears on my screen. Am I going to be the one to crack the case? But he literally says nothing. He just keeps shaking his head no, no, no. Then he says, "Are we done here?" which seems impressively ballsy, and in the blink of an eye, he slides out of the frame and is gone. Ebony is doing the interview with Leigha. I guess she feels me leering over her shoulder.

"I do not need your help," she signs. And then adds, "OK, I do need some help." The tape just shows Leigha crying, crying, crying. If she is saying any actual words, they are unintelligible.

"I don't know if I can help you with this," I sign.

"Not from you," she signs. "From Smiley." I make my quizzical-eyebrow face. She explains, "Obviously, she is crying hysterically. But she was not at first. I'm trying to figure out what they asked that set her off. I cannot quite see the question."

"The detective was off camera. Nobody can help you with that," I sign.

"Look closely," she points. "See the reflection in the window?" I see. Hawley's reflected gaze is fairly clear. I had missed it. Ebony *is* a freaking girl detective. What else don't I know about her? "Does it zoom in?" she asks. I indicate that I will get Devon.

I go out into the hall and find him keeping watch through a little pair of binoculars that totally aren't necessary. The hall is empty. I tap him on the shoulder, and he jumps about four feet in the air and then tries to play it off like he hadn't just shrieked, though even I know that he did. His eyebrows tell me he is asking if I found anything. "W-E N-E-E-D Y-O-U-R H-E-L-P," I sign. He darts into the room. Ebony has paused the footage and is pointing at the reflection of Hawley in the window at the corner of the screen.

She then says something out loud to Devon. He looks shocked. I am sort of surprised too. I had forgotten that she actually can speak and that she isn't afraid of "sounding deaf" like I am. But her back is half turned, so I can't see what she had said. I tap her on the shoulder and make an angry gesture. "I said," she signs, "zoom in." Then she adds, "Don't get your panties in a twist, Will Halpin."

Devon picks up his handkerchief and works the controls to zoom in on Hawley's face. It is blurry and Hawley has that stellar mustache, but, amazingly, we can see his lips pretty clearly. Devon plays the footage. And when we realize what Hawley says, Ebony and I stare at each other, gaping at the screen, rewinding a few times to be sure, gaping some more. Devon's eyes grow huge. "What?" he signs. "What? What? What?" Ebony and I both write in our notebook the question that it really seems Hawley asked: "The baby that you are carrying—is it his?"

Devon's jaw basically falls on the floor. And then he starts pressing buttons like a madman, shutting the units off as fast as he can. He indicates that we should duck down by violently motioning to the floor. We dive against the wall by the front door while he shuts off the lights.

We sit in the dark in a collective three-part panic. I put my beard on in case I need to be disguised. (Maybe I just like the beard?) Ebony and I are elbow to elbow, hunched by the front door, while Devon cowers a few feet away. There is only a tiny bit of light showing through the window in the door. I have a sick sensation like I had at the mine, like a chunk of time is being torn from my life. Neither Ebony nor I have any idea what is happening. We have to put all of our trust in the Smileyman, and I have the odd, unbidden thought that maybe there really is no noise out there and Devon has just crafted this as an elaborate ruse to see how *much* we trust him.

I almost jump out of my skin when I feel a sudden vibration against my thigh. I am getting a message on my Crony. Devon and I had been trying to include Ebony in the conversations all day, so we hadn't been using them. It is, however, the perfect way to communicate stealthily in the dark. The pale light of the tiny screen illuminates the words just enough so I can see what he writes:

Smiley_Man3ooo: Chet, someone is out there.

HamburgerHalpin: i figured. who is it frank? lucille?

Smiley_Man3ooo: No. Weird thing is, I think it's a student.

HamburgerHalpin: what the hell? who?

Smiley_Man3ooo: Unless I'm mistaken, it's Dwight Carlson.

Before I can even process what this could mean, Ebony reaches over and grabs the Crony from me. She reads the screen and wrestles me away while typing. I end up reading over her shoulder.

HamburgerHalpin: who the hell is dwight carlson?

Smiley_Man3ooo: Chet, he's in all your classes.

HamburgerHalpin: chet's not typing--it's me, the black rose.

Smiley_Man3ooo: What?

HamburgerHalpin: dev, it's me--ebony. "in search of the black rose" was my favorite nancy drew book. why should i be the only one without a code name?

Smiley_Man3ooo: I apologize for the oversight! And while I agree that you should have a nickname, and concur that the Black Rose is an awesome choice, I'm just not sure now is the right time to be discussing it. We're sort of in the middle of a tense situation here!

HamburgerHalpin: who is this carlson?

Smiley_Man3ooo: Just a kid from class.

HamburgerHalpin: is he big?

Smiley_Man3ooo: Nah.

HamburgerHalpin: tough?

Smiley_Man3ooo: Nah--my size.

HamburgerHalpin: as cute as u?

Smiley_Man3ooo: What?

HamburgerHalpin: ok, here's what we're going to do. i'll run into the hallway and disable carlson. when i give the signal, make a run for it. don't forget to alert the fat one.

Smiley_Man3ooo: What do you mean, "disable"?

But the Black Rose is already peeking out the window at the pacing Dwight Carlson. When his back is turned, she takes a deep breath and makes her move. In a sudden, powerful motion, she tears open the door and leaps on Dwight's back. She then busts out a move somewhere between a judo throw and a hockey check. I watch in stunned amazement as Ebony pulls Dwight's jacket over his head and pushes him to his knees. The jacket covers his eyes, effectively blinding him. She grabs the fingers of his left hand and pulls them backward while placing her knee in between his shoulder blades. Then she gives the signal. Devon grabs "the fat one" and pulls me out the door.

We are running—running as fast as our feet can carry us— up the stairs, down the hall, and out of the building. Like a real-life cartoon character, I almost literally run out of my clothes. The button on my pants has helpfully popped off, so I have to hold them up with one hand while chasing after Devon. Everything is a blur. We sprint across the parking lot, cruise past the teachers' cars, cut through the soccer fields, and have never been so happy to see the Smileywagon. There Devon and I stand with our hands on the hood, trying to catch our breath. It is all quite beyond comprehension but, once we stop to think about it, sort of hilarious. Devon cracks a smile between heavy breaths and then, seeing me grinning through my fake beard and busted pants, lets out an uncontrollable guffaw. I immediately find myself laughing until tears—literal tears of chubby, wet joy—run from my eyes. A beautiful moment. Is there anything more sublime than two friends sharing a laugh at the absurdly weird and dangerous world? I know Devon is thinking the same exact thing. And then our moods change as suddenly and ominously as a clock striking twelve. At once we both realize that Ebony is nowhere to be found.

CHAPTER THIRTY-SEVEN

What happened to her? Is she caught? Lost? Is Dwight Carlson a secret karate master who was able to reverse her hold and now has her pinned to the ground in the school basement? Everything unlikely seems to be happening. I want to send Devon a text, but Ebony still has my Crony. I can't find my notebook. Did I leave it in the janitor's office? Surely someone will find it. We will get busted for trespassing and hacking into the surveillance system. Worse: someone could be reading all my notes! I had little comments about everyone. It is extremely embarrassing to imagine it falling into the wrong hands. Which is to say, anyone's hands other than my own.

I am going to try to finger-spell all this to Devon when suddenly his face lights up. He grabs his Crony. Ebony is sending him a text! I squeeze in next to him so I can read the tiny screen.

Def4Life: d, it's ebony. log in to im--i'm def4life.

Smiley_Man3ooo: OMG! Are you OK?

Def4Life: u won't believe what happened.

Smiley_Man3ooo: What?

Def4Life: while i was taking out carlson, your principal came down the hall!

Smiley_Man3ooo: Kroener?

Def4Life: i guess. he saw me fighting carlson so he tried to punch me!

Smiley_Man3ooo: Oh no!

Def4Life: but i blocked the punch and put him in an armlock.

Smiley_Man3ooo: Whoa!

Def4Life: i could have broken his arm, but he started begging for mercy.

Smiley_Man3ooo: Did you let him go?

Def4Life: i told him that the only way i'd let him go was if he made out with carlson.

Smiley_Man3ooo: !?!?!?!

Def4Life: so then he totally started kissing carlson.

Smiley_Man3ooo: Yowza!?!?!?!

Def4Life: and i was like "use your tongues!" and
they were totally going at it for like five minutes!

Before Devon can type "!?!?!?!" yet again, he looks up like
he has heard something. He makes a sheepish face and points.
There is Ebony, laughing and typing as she saunters across the
parking lot. I sign a few pointed words at her. She signs back
that I shouldn't "slow her roll" and explains that she was only a
minute behind us because she went back to retrieve our notebooks. "Nancy would never have left anything behind," she
signs. She then takes my notebook out of her pocket and begins flipping through the pages. "Some pretty weird stuff in
here, Halpin," she signs. I tell her to mind her own business
while I reach to grab it from her. "Leigha equals hot?" she
signs. "Scuzzy guy loves his fingers? And why would you want to
stay away from Devon?" I sign a few more choice threats before
she tosses the book to me. Then I go to grab my Crony back
when it starts vibrating. Ebony doesn't let me answer it. She
keeps typing while somehow avoiding my attempts to grab the
device. Freaking karate master.

Smiley_Man3ooo: Umm, hello, guys? I'm still here.

Def4Life: sorry, that was rude of us.

Smiley_Man3ooo: Did you leave Carlson and
Kroener making out?

Def4Life: omg, u r 2 gullible, smileyman.

Smiley_Man3ooo: Oh, I mean . . . I knew you were kidding.

Def4Life: riiiiiiiiiiiight.

Smiley_Man3ooo: So what were you and Chet signing about just now? Looked like some pretty interesting signs.

Def4Life: i was explaining that i went back for the notebooks. most of the rest of the signs were curses.

Smiley_Man3ooo: Hey, can you teach me? I do believe I would enjoy sign-swearing.

Def4Life: that pisses me off--the only thing hearing people want to know in asl is how to curse.

Smiley_Man3ooo: Oh dear, I am so sorry!

Def4Life: ah, ur lucky ur cute, smiley. i'll teach ya. but we should probably get out of here. i think carlson went for help. also i have to get to the dojo.

Ebony signs, "Shotgun," then throws my Crony to me. She climbs in the front of the Smileywagon while I clump into the back, exhausted and dazed. I finally get my pants to stay on. Must nap soon. Devon's lurching driving is worse than normal as he tries out all the new swear signs. Ebony signs it first, then he repeats.

"Bastard."

"Bastard."

"Piss off, wanker."

"Piss off, wanker."

I hope a deaf person drives up next to us and looks in the window. They would die.

"Man love! Man love!"

"Man love! Man love!"

"Eat shit, fat cow."

"Eat shit, fat cow."

Hey!

Then she starts teaching him a few weird ones, which he does wrong. He keeps accidentally signing "Lesbian Jew" for some reason. "Lesbian Jew! Lesbian Jew! Lesbian Jew!" I lean back and doze off with a smile on my face.

CHAPTER THIRTY-EIGHT

I am startled by the vibrations of my Crony and wake up feeling lost. I slowly recognize my surroundings as the backseat of the Smileywagon. Devon is sitting in front like my chauffeur. Ebony is gone. We are parked somewhere I don't recognize.

Smiley_Man3ooo: So, do deaf people have superb strength in their other senses? Like how blind people hear really well?

HamburgerHalpin: what? where the hell are we? and if you say "trust the smileyman" i'll yank your ponytail

Smiley_Man3ooo: I've just been driving around thinking about what we uncovered. Can you believe that Leigha is pregnant?

HamburgerHalpin: i can and i can't at the same time. know what i mean?

Smiley_Man3ooo: I think so. Pretty crazy. So, do you have extrasensory powers?

HamburgerHalpin: i never really thought about it

Smiley_Man3ooo: Well, you do seem to be quite apt with your sense of taste.

HamburgerHalpin: i'll handle the fat jokes smileyman

Smiley_Man3ooo: Sorry.

HamburgerHalpin: now that you mention it i do sort of smell good

Smiley_Man3ooo: Take it from me: you do not smell good.

HamburgerHalpin: i mean smell well u grammar nazi.

Smiley_Man3ooo: Sorry.

HamburgerHalpin: u r mr funnyman today huh?

Smiley_Man3ooo: Sorry.

HamburgerHalpin: my eyesight is quite keen

Smiley_Man3ooo: Perfect!

HamburgerHalpin: y?

Smiley_Man3ooo: Your eagle-eyed vision is just what we need to take the next step in our investigation. We're getting close! You are sure to find some clues when we go back to the mine.

HamburgerHalpin: we r going back to the mine?

Smiley_Man3ooo: We r.

HamburgerHalpin: when?

Smiley_Man3ooo: Right now. We just have to go pick up my dad.

HamburgerHalpin: y?

Smiley_Man3ooo: I figure that having a man in blue along will open some doors for us. Especially since the mine is still closed to the public. I made some calls to the manager--a guy named Albert Fitzsimmons--and he agreed to meet us there to let us in.

HamburgerHalpin: when did u do all this?

Smiley_Man3ooo: While you napped, you lazy turd. Always trust the Smileyman!

HamburgerHalpin: wow

Smiley_Man3ooo: And one more thing: I'm pretty sure we won't get reception down in the mine, so we can't text. But I told my dad to bring some whiteboards and dry-erase markers. Let's solve this thing!

HamburgerHalpin: the smileyman does think of everything

We drive to the police station. Mr. Smiley is sitting on a bench outside whistling through his big mustache. As soon as he sees the Smileywagon, he indicates that we should park. Devon parks, we get out, and Mr. S. leads us to a cruiser secured for the mission. I get in the back, an act that brings on the beginnings of another claustrophobic panic attack. Before I freak too much, we are on the road, moving quickly. Mr. S. even turns on the siren (or so Devon tells me, turning around and signing happily through the Plexiglas) so we don't have to wait in traffic.

After a brisk drive, we are at the mine, revisiting the place that just a few days ago was the scene of such chaos but now stands as silent as a tomb. Or so I surmise. The news vehicles have moved on to a fresher tragedy. The large parking lot is empty, with the exception of three vehicles. One, a van painted with ads for Happy Memory Coal Mine, obviously belongs to the manager. Another is just like ours—a police cruiser from the same department. The third is a sleek, black, official-looking vehicle with darkened windows. As Mr. S. parks the cruiser and we head toward the door, I check out the license plate. It identifies the black car as belonging to an employee of the federal government.

I jab Devon with my elbow and point toward it. He makes a

stunned face and then says something to his dad. Mr. S. says something back, and then Devon turns to me and finger-spells out the three letters I had already suspected: "F-B-I."

So the feds have shown up in our sleepy little town. Is this because Pat's dad is a powerful man with powerful friends? And powerful enemies? Could there really be something to the idea that Pat's death was somehow connected to the scandals in Congress? Was his dad going to rat somebody out? Were these powerful people scared enough that they would kill a high school kid to silence Mr. Chambers? Was a hired hit man really involved? I have to remind myself that the people on TheTruthIsNot.com also believed that pennies are still in circulation only because they each contain tiny radio-frequency-identification chips that allow the government to track the movements of every citizen. Of course, the reason they believed that was because *someone* planted that rumor in their "talkback" forum, but still . . .

Devon, Mr. S., and I approach the front entrance to the mine, where the giant fake rat leers at us with its yellow eyes. Mr. S. knocks on the closed door. When no one answers, he just lets himself in. We see the manager of the mine—that Albert Fitzsimmons—first. I recognize Fitzsimmons as one of the mine employees who was running around the parking lot in a blithering panic. Fitzsimmons is a beefy man with a shiny head and an unusual row of glittering earrings in his left ear. He is obviously deep in conversation. One of the men with whom he is speaking is Detective Hawley, and the third guy is clearly FBI. Tall and wrapped in a dark black coat, which bulges menacingly around a belt that presumably holds all manner of deadly weapons, he stares down at Fitzsimmons with an unblinking intensity. His tightly cropped mustache slowly rises and falls as his jaws intently work over a piece of gum like a relentlessly grilled suspect.

Mr. S., who has apparently decided to just go for it, barges right in. I watch his lips, curious as to what he is going to say.

"Fitzy?" he asks the seated manager. "Smiley here. County P.D. And these boys here are helping me look into a few things. We (*something something*) on the phone?"

Hawley looks furious. Mr. Smiley gives no sign of even recognizing that he is there. Fitzsimmons is momentarily baffled. His eyes narrow and his head shakes, setting off a rippling cascade of neck fat. And then he breaks into a huge smile. I can't see his response, but he is obviously pleased Mr. Smiley has given him some sort of way to get out of being interrogated by the scary FBI guy. The scary FBI guy, on the other hand, looks tightly peeved. Very tightly peeved. He has words with Hawley, then comes over to us, grabs Mr. Smiley by the elbow—not in a mean way, but still aggressively—and whispers something into his ear.

"Well, I guess we'll be going then," says Mr. Smiley (or something like that), and turns to the door.

Devon is furious.

"Dad!" he says. "We came all the way out here. Just please let us (*something something*) for a few minutes!"

"Sorry, son, but the nice agent here has some business with Mr. Fitzsimmons. And this is still a crime scene. Or, uh, a (*something something*) scene of a possible crime. And, yeah, well, uh, (*something something*)."

Mr. Smiley turns to the door. Devon looks at me with a strange expression. Then he winks. And starts to cry.

In just a minute, he has whipped up a tornado of full-on tears, sputtering and spitting like a baby at a funeral. I can't quite see the words, but I think he says "best friend" in there somewhere. Is he claiming that Pat was his best friend? And that he needs to go visit the death site because of his grief? He pulls a flower—one of my mom's crumpled mums—from his pocket and says, "I have to mark the place where my friend perished." Man, is this effective! Mr. Smiley, Albert Fitzsimmons, and even the tough FBI guy and the evil Detective Hawley all look crushed. It is like they are dealing with a whimpering puppy. While the adults have a little discussion about how exactly to get Devon to stop his weeping, Devon starts signing to me with his right hand while his left hand holds the flower and wipes away torrents of tears.

"D-O-N-T J-U-D-G-E M-E, M-Y G-O-O-D M-A-N. B-U-T I K-N-E-W T-H-I-S W-O-U-L-D W-O-R-K."

It does. Mr. Fitzsimmons gives us some of those lantern hats out of the bin and has some words with Mr. Smiley while the other two men sulk. I don't see what Fitzy has to say, but he seems to be pointing out the areas we are allowed into and the spots that are absolutely off-limits. He then shows us the way down the tracks back to where we had taken our tour. Fitzy and the FBI guy return to their tense conversation while Hawley looks like a volcano ready to blow. Mr. S. follows Devon looking bemused. Devon practically skips down the dusty path.

I am so impressed with Devon's performance and so

weirded out by this strange scene that I momentarily forget to wonder what exactly we are doing here in the first place. All Devon had said was that we were going to look for clues. But what could we hope to find that everyone else had missed? Surely every inch of the old mine has been combed and examined with the highest-tech devices available? All Devon and I have is our little notebooks and my so-called super-vision. Some deaf people do have extrakeen vision, it is true, but I am not going to pick up anything the experts had missed with their zoom lenses and laser scanner things.

Devon pretends that he is going to place the flower at the area where Pat had died, steering clear of the area still outlined in police tape, which the FBI guy had warned us about. He signs to me that I should "look for" clues. He does the actual sign for "look for," which is a funny gesture almost like you're peering through an imaginary telescope. Impressive. It seems that the thing Devon wants to do most is to take measurements (yes, he brought a protractor) to calculate the angle at which Pat fell. But why is he wasting our time trying to prove that Pat had been pushed? The professionals had already determined that! I get sick of watching him squint and calculate, so I cruise back up the path.

I walk to a spot where I can watch Detective Hawley and Mr. Smiley arguing. Hawley looks like his head might explode, while Mr. S. just holds his palms up to the ceiling and grins an annoying grin.

After walking just a little farther, I realize I am right near the spot where Miner Carl mentioned Dummy Halpin. I had taken that to mean that we were very close to the place where Dummy had perished. On the field trip, I was too distracted to think about what Miner Carl really meant. But this is . . . the spot. *The* spot. I am glad I am alone, free of my classmates and Devon and everyone else. So what am I feeling? A connection? Could there be an electric aura passed through the years, some feeling of the germ that became the virus of my life?

I am zoning out and feeling sorry for myself, feeling sad for Dummy and everything, looking at nothing in particular, when my eyes fall on something. A few feet up in the wall of solid rock is a rough outline that looks like nothing so much as a door. Not a real door—just a natural displacement of rock making the mouth of an entrance to someplace. To where? I check to see if Devon or Mr. Smiley or anyone is looking. Nope. It isn't easy to see—the rock wall is covered by a shadow—but if you skip across like an agile mountain goat (or like a semiagile walrus), you are suddenly in a little passage. I stick my head into the mouth of the pitch-black entrance.

I flip on the light of my miner's hat and see, to my surprise, what looks like a shadowy tunnel. I pull myself in. And therein recur both the panic of claustrophobia and the thrill of discovery. A secret passage! And something tells me, an instinct, that many years ago my ancestor, the original Will Halpin, had been in this exact spot.

Or maybe, just maybe, it is these words, clawed into the rock: DUMMY WAS HERE.

CHAPTER THIRTY-NINE

I rub my eyes. Still there. I rub my eyes again. Yep. I slap myself a few times with the palm of my dirty hand, close my eyes tight, and then open them again. Still there, and now my face stings.

I crawl ahead a little farther—another D.H. scrawled into the wall. And then another. Why did he do this? Was he leaving a trail? For me to follow? And then I had this crazy thought: What if Dummy never died? What if he escaped? Didn't I read that they never found a body? What if he pulled himself up into this little passageway and let everyone think that he died? But why would he do that?

I follow the path farther, straining to fit down the narrow passageway and trying as hard as I can not to think about what will happen if I get stuck. As I proceed, the passage does get somewhat roomier. I can't stand up, or even crouch, but I can get on my hands and knees, which is way preferable to the belly crawl I had been doing. I am moving along with relative ease for probably a hundred feet, following the D.H. markings in the rock, chasing the ghost of Dummy Halpin. And then the passage comes to a fork. Two choices. I can turn to the right into the dark and unknown or to the left into the dark and unknown. Of course, I can also scamper back to safety. But, instead, I sit, hunched, looking from right to left, from left to right. To the left there seems to be the tiniest sliver of light above an incline, while the right is pure blackness. And, just because that's the kind of guy I am, I go for the black.

I squeeze my bulk down the rightward passage. Will I find something wonderful, like hidden treasure or diamonds? Or something awful—perhaps the skeleton of Dummy Halpin? I crawl for what seems like forever through the choking darkness. And what do I find? Devon Smiley.

Dev isn't in the passage like I am; he is still hanging out near the ledge taking measurements. But I have taken a path, apparently, from the spot where Dummy had died around to another opening right near where Pat died. I emerge like a turtle, sticking my head out of the cave behind the DO NOT CROSS taped-off area, and see Devon. I am close enough to grab his ponytail. So I do. And I really would have liked to have heard the scream, because, judging from his face, he is scared to the point of involuntary urination.

I get a little scared too, realizing I am sort of near that ledge, so I scooch back, crawling in reverse. Fueled by fear and guided by the blazes of Dummy's markings illuminated by my headlamp, I crawl out to where I entered and walk the path back around to where I started. In a minute I am behind Devon, close enough to tap him on the shoulder. He screams again. I laugh.

"What are you?" he writes with a shaking hand on the little whiteboard he had brought so we could converse. "A magic person?" This last part he doesn't write but signs. The guy really has been practicing his signs. Who (other than Camp Arrowhead alumni) learns compound words like that? ("Magician" is made up of "magic" and "person.") Impressive indeed.

I nod. And then I write on the whiteboard he had handed me. "I am the Hefty Houdini."

He laughs but still looks somewhat panicked. "How *did* you get over there?" he writes. Italics in handwriting?

I write it out, and Devon's eyes light up. Does he share my vague excitement about this twist in the Dummy Halpin ghost story? No. What really gets him buzzing is the discovery of a secret passage.

He scribbles, "It's just like in the Hardy Boys' *The House on the Cliff*! It was one of the first ones Chet was in!"

"Are you seriously talking Hardy Boys?"

"Well, it is a pretty interesting coincidence."

"Devon, focus on this: I may have just found some sort of clue that my ancestor—my namesake, the original Will Halpin—maybe didn't die but found a passage out and escaped!"

"But anyone could have written that," Devon scribbles. "Maybe they were just honoring him by writing his name near the spot where he died."

"Yeah, but . . . ," I start to write. Geezo. I hadn't thought of

205

it that way. Why was I so sure Dummy wrote those notes? I am suddenly deflated.

"Perhaps we should also consider," Devon writes, "that whoever killed Pat could have used that same secret passage."

True. But maybe . . .

CHAPTER FORTY

Mr. Smiley comes back down the path with the FBI guy and Albert Fitzsimmons. All three wear uneasy and sweaty expressions. Mr. Smiley taps the back of his watch with his index finger, another one of those signs that hearing people do that actually is real sign language. Time to go. We head back up to the mouth of the mine. Fitzsimmons can't resist trying to get us to spend some money in the gift shop, and Devon can't resist buying another "future diamond." Sigh.

As we make our way back through the parking lot, I point to something far off in the distance. When Devon stops to look, I rush to the car so I can get the front seat. We immediately start texting as Mr. Smiley drives toward home.

Smiley_Man3ooo: What were you pointing at?

HamburgerHalpin: u idiot--i was only trying to distract you so i could get the front seat

Smiley_Man3ooo: Ha-ha. So it was a pretty productive trip, huh? And just think: you didn't want to go.

HamburgerHalpin: i'm still not sure what we figured out chambers-wise. i hate to ask: how were your calculations?

Smiley_Man3ooo: Pat was definitely pushed.

HamburgerHalpin: duh

Smiley_Man3ooo: Well, yeah, but I was trying to figure out the force. What I found is that I don't think he was pushed by somebody very strong.

HamburgerHalpin: how do u figure?

Smiley_Man3ooo: The arc of his fall shows an acute angle--he landed almost right at the base. If someone really strong hit him or shoved him, he would have landed much farther out.

HamburgerHalpin: u did all that with your protractor?

Smiley_Man3ooo: Never leave home without it!

HamburgerHalpin: nerd alert!

Smiley_Man3000: Yeah, so, any new ideas on suspects?

HamburgerHalpin: any new ideas on where we're going to lunch?

Smiley_Man3000: Oh, Chet, you are ever the growing boy.

HamburgerHalpin: just ask yr dad if we can get some burgers. chet can't think on an empty stomach

Mr. Smiley reluctantly takes us to a diner for burgers and sodas. We try to text while eating, but Mr. S. scolds us to put away "those damn toys." I remember that Devon got mine in a suspicious fashion from the police evidence room. Does Mr. Smiley know this? Is he afraid that we will be seen with it? Running into Detective Hawley really seems to have spooked him. So, apparently even cops like Hawley and Smiley have their own problems with hierarchies and rankings. Is the whole damn world like high school?

I try to sign a joke to Devon over our meal, but he is confused when I say, "You should never talk with your hands full." I think he gets "talk" and "hands" (pretty obvious ones), but I guess joking in another language is kind of hard. We left the whiteboards in the car and so concentrate on eating as fast as we can. It is clear that Mr. Smiley wants to get out of there. Eating quickly and feeling nervous sort of make my stomach sick.

A fart slips out, which I hope is a silent one. Yes, it is one of the great burdens of the hearing-impaired that we do not know who else is aware of the gas we pass. I think about trying another joke—that old chestnut "Why do farts smell? So deaf people won't feel left out"—but it would take forever to finger-spell it.

We finish our meal and head home. Mr. Smiley pulls into my driveway, I hop out, and Devon holds up his fist as if to say, "Keep up the fight" for some reason. The mailman walks up, delivering a large envelope. I take it from him and see the local newspaper's name as the return address. Ah, the obituary and photo I had requested from their archives. I rip open the package and stare at the picture, like a hungry man sizing up a rib eye. As soon as my eyes fall on it, I am overwhelmed by a strong sense of recognition—although where could I have seen him before? There was no picture in our textbook, and our family doesn't have any Dummy portraits proudly displayed. "Hello," I sign to the picture. "I am Will Halpin. You are Will Halpin. I am Will Halpin. You are Will Halpin." Just standing in the driveway, conversing with the dead.

Mom and Dad are at work, and the house feels big and lonely. I prop the photo on my desk and halfheartedly try to do my homework next to this ancient picture of a grinning Dummy Halpin clowning around for an old camera circa 1900. I spend some time on Leigha's profile page. But this just makes me feel queasy and anxious.

I tell myself that it is a nice day so, what the hell, I should just go out walking, feel the sun, hear the birds sing (kidding).

It is said that walking helps clear the brain, lets you figure stuff out, though my brain can be cleared quite fine, thank you very much, by sitting on the couch. Still, it feels good to move, and I get a leash for Ace and bring him along. A dog is a good excuse for taking a walk, maybe spying a little. Ace appreciates it, wagging happily alongside and whizzing on everything in sight. We walk up past the barn next to our house and into the new housing development. All around this old coal town, big houses have been springing up like weeds after a rain. You blink and forty-seven mansions sit where there used to be woods. Gone are the trees I climbed as a boy. Gone are the innocent afternoons spent romping carefree through the woods. Gone are the . . . Ha-ha, I'm totally making that up. I never spent any time in the woods. And only recently have I romped.

I take some little side roads, snaking lazily down newly paved streets with names like Bougainvillea and Abronia. I know these are names of plants, but they also sound like possible types of venereal disease. As I puff along, I suddenly feel my eyes bug out of my head like a stunned skunk in an old cartoon. There, sitting on the step in front of one of the new homes on Abronia Lane, is Leigha Pennington. I blink and rub my eyes. Yep, it is really her. Well, I sorta did know that she lived on Abronia. (What? It is in the phone book—hardly a secret.)

She doesn't see me, so I watch her carefully. She is barefoot, wearing a green army jacket over a tan shirt and ripped jeans, and sipping on a bottle of ginger ale. She is, in a gesture that is very cute if sort of gross, letting her fuzzy black dog lick the bottle. This dog, who I recognize from Leigha's Web page picture, alternates between sharing the soda and sitting at her feet like a sentry guarding an entrance. I stop in my tracks and watch this private scene, which should be happy yet isn't. Too much of life is like that.

She's not smoking. See, if she was, I could go up to her and pretend to bum a smoke. (The sign for smoking is: you basically just pretend to be smoking.) But then what? Sit there in silence while she laughs at me for coughing my lungs out? (I have never smoked before. Cigarettes, I mean. I have smoked a ham. And a turkey or two.) Also, that she isn't smoking is a good thing since she is pregnant. Pregnant. Geez.

Should I flee? But before I have the chance to spin and show off my world-class sprinting skills, I am spotted. The dog cocks its head and spies Ace. They are both barking at one another, scoping each other out. Leigha then cocks her head too, in a gesture oddly similar to her pet's. She exhales a huge sigh and waves me over.

I point to my chest as if to ask, "Me?"

She gestures to the empty street with an upturned palm as if to ask, "You see anybody else around?"

I do not.

And so I walk slowly toward her, hoping that Leigha has a soft heart and that her dog won't use me for a chew toy. My heart rocketing in my chest, I stand a few feet from her in the dirt of her unfinished lawn. The dogs sniff each other. I pat Ace to let him know that everything is OK. But is it?

Leigha waves hi. I wave back. And then she does the informal sign for writing. Is she asking me if I have some paper or maybe a whiteboard? I shake my head. Then she shakes her head. What are we talking about? She points at me and scribbles in the air again. And then points to herself and nods. I have gotten rather good at figuring out such random sign language and am pretty sure she means "I got your note." I nod, trying to stay cool, actually feeling like I might blow a fuse.

And then she pauses for a second and shakes her head. And she doesn't have to say another word. I know that she precisely means "No, we can't be friends. No, I won't go out with you. No, you and me can never be anything. Ever."

I hang my head and turn to leave. Then I stop. I face her again. I have one last shot. I pick up a stick from the yard. The dogs perk at the stick, excited for a potential game of fetch. But I use it to write in the dirt.

"I KNOW YOUR PAIN."

She looks down at the letters with a weary gaze and shakes her head again. "No," she mouths. "You have no idea."

"I KNOW YOUR SECRET," I write. I feel like if she just gives me a chance, she will see that I can be a friend. I can listen even if I can't listen. I can understand her. I can understand everything. But before I even have the chance to explain any more of this, she reacts to my words with a look of fury and . . . maybe fear? She scrapes her foot across the dirt, erasing my message in one swift kick. Then she hops up and runs inside her house, slamming the door so hard that I feel the whoosh of warm air from inside. Am I really that repulsive?

Leigha's dog still is staring at me, waiting for the stick to fly from my hand. I have no idea what else to do, so I hand it to him. He takes it excitedly, and Ace grabs the other half. They snap it in two, gnawing the bark, reducing it in seconds to a slobbery, fractured mess. I am just like this stupid stick. Chewed up and spit out.

Ace and I turn back down Abronia and walk home.

CHAPTER FORTY-ONE

I am farting around online a bit, though it feels hollow. Inciting anger by insisting that global warming is awesome because the world would be better without cashmere scarves and stupid polar bears just doesn't seem that fun. An IM window jumps up.

> Smiley_Man3ooo: How does the evening find you, Chet?
>
> HamburgerHalpin: hey frank. i feel . . . what's the word? glum?
>
> Smiley_Man3ooo: Why is that? All in all, it was a good day.

I cannot tell Devon what happened with Leigha. I just can't.

HamburgerHalpin: i'm not sure i made the right choice switching schools

Smiley_Man3ooo: You're doing great!

HamburgerHalpin: well it's too late anyway. ur stuck with me. i'm here now. i'm in it to win it

Smiley_Man3ooo: "In it to win it"?

HamburgerHalpin: isn't that what all the kids say?

Smiley_Man3ooo: Sure, Will. All us hepcat kids say that.

HamburgerHalpin: :)

Smiley_Man3ooo: Want a ride to school tomorrow?

HamburgerHalpin: would love one . . . i wish i could drive

Smiley_Man3ooo: You can borrow my car if you want.

HamburgerHalpin: i don't have a license

Smiley_Man3ooo: Oh, is that because of your . . . condition?

HamburgerHalpin: i'm not blind

Smiley_Man3ooo: I meant your . . . other . . . condition.

HamburgerHalpin: ?

Smiley_Man3ooo: I was delicately implying that you might be too massive to fit behind an average steering wheel--as a joke, my good man.

HamburgerHalpin: r u finished?

Smiley_Man3ooo: Yeah, sorry. You were saying?

HamburgerHalpin: they don't offer driver's ed at the deaf school. and i'd really need an interpreter

Smiley_Man3ooo: I could teach you!

HamburgerHalpin: yeah but dude this is driving. and ok no offense but the tru story is that your driving scares me

Smiley_Man3ooo: I am an excellent driver!

HamburgerHalpin: riiiight

Smiley_Man3ooo: Hey!

HamburgerHalpin: well i did the math and it would only cost a few grand to hire an interpreter but our county is 2 cheap

Smiley_Man3ooo: Plenty of money for football, though!

HamburgerHalpin: yeah

Smiley_Man3ooo: Is that really what has you down?

HamburgerHalpin: that and this whole dummy halpin thing. it's just so . . . i can't explain

Smiley_Man3ooo: I think I get it. It's this important part of your personal history that your parents never told you. You had to find out in a history book that a family member shared your name and condition.

HamburgerHalpin: thnx again 4 everything u know

Smiley_Man3ooo: Nothing at all! But I know that passageway meant a lot to you for your personal history, but I also feel like it means everything for our investigation. I just can't figure out how. . . .

HamburgerHalpin: but why do you think my parents kept all the dummy stuff from me really?

Smiley_Man3ooo: I hate to sound like a giant dork, but . . .

HamburgerHalpin: it's never stopped you before

Smiley_Man3ooo: That sounds like a question you need to ask your parents.

Stupid Devon is right. I need to talk with stupid Ken and Mona. And I need to try to do it without smashing any lamps or storming off to bed without supper. Especially that last one.

I head down to again wait for them in the living room, holding the picture of Dummy Halpin, but not looking for a fight, just a conversation. Just a chance to learn a little more about our family, who I am. I can't be too pissed at them for not being honest with me. Not when I haven't been honest with them either.

When Ken and Mona, uh, Mom and Dad, come through the front door, I decide to lay it all on the line. If only I had time to prepare a file folder like Devon would have, to let them know everything in plain printed English. As it is, I just sign slowly and simply so Mom can get it all and translate for Dad. I decide to give him a little bit of a break for not being fluent. Watching Devon make the effort has reminded me how hard sign language really is.

"How was your day?" Mom asks. She of course doesn't expect a real answer, no more than someone does when they say "How's it hanging?"

"Awful," I say, a sign that involves a double-hand gesture but is mainly communicated by making a sad, terrible face.

At first she thinks I mean because of all the big stuff—Prefontaine, Porkrinds, Chambers, et cetera.

"No," I sign, snapping my fingers and also shaking my head for Dad's sake. "It is more than that. I am having a hard time at school." I explain about how crappy people are to me sometimes, how the teachers don't know what to do with me, and how awful I feel most of the time. I stop short of telling them about the investigation or my visit with Leigha.

Mom immediately suggests that I go back to the deaf school. I am not quite sure why, but I don't feel like that is the answer.

I shake my head no, no, no.

I take out the envelope and show them the picture. I tell them about my research and the second trip to the mine. And then I ask, "Can't you tell me something more about our family?" And something about the sign for "family"—a variation on "group" where you sort of make a circle as if to say "all of us"— strikes me as so . . . something that I almost want to cry.

Dad tells me that he's done some research of his own. Really?! He takes out a scrapbook whose pages show a family tree and a few faded black-and-white pictures of stout men and women. Some have big ears and beards, with serious eyes blazing at the camera.

Above his own name on the tree, however, are just names. No pictures, no facts.

I point to the empty spaces. Why not more?

Dad looks away. He takes a deep breath. He gestures for me to follow him upstairs. Mom starts to follow, but Dad does the karate chop that means "stop." It's to be just me and him, I guess. Man-to-man. Mom looks a little sad.

We enter the attic. Dad pulls a chain, and an overhead bulb flickers to life. I see old books and games, even a drum kit from that weird phase when I decided I wanted to be a musician. I could feel the vibrations of the bass drum and looked really cool twirling the drumsticks. Why did I give that up?

Various other Halpin artifacts sit in unsorted piles. It's clear Dad has been up here on a personal mission, digging through our history. He picks up a dusty metal box, inserts a key on a long yellow ribbon, and pops it open. "This is all I have," he says, gesturing so I get the point. The box contains a picture of

his parents. His father, Grandpa Halpin, was one ample ancestor. As Dad shows me the picture, I laugh because Dad remem-
bers a sign for "fat" that really is hilarious—you use your thumb
and pinkie to make a little chubber waddle around in the air.

Then Dad makes the sign for "drunk," which you do by trying to take a drink but missing your face. It kind of looks like
you're throwing a punch. And then he does punch his hand.
This is, not surprisingly, the sign for "punch."

I don't have to say the question. I just raise my eyebrows.
Dad nods.

"He hit you?"

"Yes. A lot."

He mimes taking off his belt, and I just shake my head.

"I got away from him, from them," Dad signs, "and never
looked back."

Well, I mean, who can blame him?

He shows me a folder with some more research into the
other Will Halpin that he'd been working on after I brought it
up and hands me some papers—a few other pictures of
Dummy from newspaper archives and a couple of different ar-
ticles. We look at them together. In one of the pictures,
Dummy has an ear trumpet and a gleam in his eye. Most of
those old dudes in those pictures have eyes black as coal. Dead
eyes. But Dummy . . . he seems mischievous, up to something. I
sign, "Thank you," and he signs it back. I'm not sure what I'm
being thanked for. We sit without saying a word.

For some reason, in that moment, several things become
clear. It is clear that if I stay at Carbon High or not, Mom and

Dad will respect my choice. And it is clear, though I am not sure how or even why, that I have to reveal what I know of the twin mysteries of Dummy Halpin and the death of Pat Chambers. I have to shine the light of truth on two guys lost in the bottom of that mine. But, first, time to go to bed.

I sleep better than I have in a long, long time.

CHAPTER FORTY-TWO

Back at school on Tuesday, I am greeted by a massive amount of Chambers tributes that had been left around the halls of Carbon High as part of the vigil the previous afternoon. There are signs, cards, even teddy bears for some reason. Outside Pat's locker, there are crosses made out of flowers, although I doubt he was a very religious guy. There are also football-shaped bouquets, which make way more sense. Someone had printed copies of his picture on red paper and stuck them on lockers, windows, doorways, and everywhere else they could reach. I guess it is supposed to make us feel better to express ourselves, but it creeps me out—his scarlet face smirking from beyond the grave.

Strangest of all, however, is the homemade T-shirt made by, you guessed it, Kevin Planders. Planders had taken an old white shirt and used Magic Markers to write COALERS on the front and

CHAMBERS 45 on the back. Then, on the sleeve, he tried to write RIP and the date Pat died, but it is hard to tell because he apparently got caught in the morning's rain.

The grief counselors are gone, but there is still a police presence in the school. As I walked through the parking lot with Devon in the morning, we noted unmarked cop cars. Devon signed, "I H-O-P-E H-A-W-L-E-Y I-S N-O-T H-E-R-E. T-H-A-T G-U-Y H-A-S I-T I-N F-O-R M-E."

Classes were supposed to return to normal, to "let the healing begin," but who are they kidding? It is way too soon to think about school. Even Arterberry is distracted. We are supposed to be learning about World War I, but he just assigns silent reading and stares out the window. What is he thinking? From the furrowing of his brow, it is clear that unpleasant thoughts are racing across his mind. Does he suspect that he is teaching a murderer in this very class? Or is he simply bummed about the disturbing revelations regarding his friend Miss Prefontaine?

I break out my little notebook. Besides for general spying on my classmates, I've been using it to sketch out my theories— even a map—of what happened at the mine. The thing is, see, I already know who killed Pat Chambers. Even if I don't want to admit it to anyone. Least of all myself.

Though such devices are prohibited in school, I crack out my Crony just on the off chance that one of those police cars belonged to Melody and she is sending me an e-mail to alert me of her presence. No such luck. What I do get, a minute after logging in, is an IM.

Smiley_Man3ooo: Hey, what are you doing on?

HamburgerHalpin: i could ask you the same thing

Smiley_Man3ooo: I don't feel like doing silent reading. Besides, Arterberry isn't even looking.

HamburgerHalpin: he seems troubled

Smiley_Man3ooo: I guess none of us can concentrate.

HamburgerHalpin: these are dark days for us coalers

Smiley_Man3ooo: You got that right. Think The Dolphin was our pusher?

HamburgerHalpin: i really don't think so. i mean obviously they were involved but she seemed really distraught when he died

Smiley_Man3ooo: But remember how mad she was when she thought he was off with Leigha? Maybe it was an act of jealousy.

HamburgerHalpin: yeah but she didn't think he was off with leigha until after he was already down

Smiley_Man3ooo: True. What about the whole CIA angle, then? It is quite a coincidence that Pat's dad was linked to something so big just as his son gets killed.

HamburgerHalpin: yeah but I think it's just that: a coincidence. the great detective said that complicated solutions rarely solve the puzzle. "when you have eliminated the impossible, whatever remains, however improbable, must be the truth"

Smiley_Man3ooo: What great detective was that? Encyclopedia Brown?

HamburgerHalpin: srsly devon what r u in third grade?

Smiley_Man3ooo: No, I get it. You're saying people usually kill for simple reasons. Back to the playing cards, then . . . and A.J. Pat gave the ace to Escapone just to further twist the knife, just to be, like, "Hey, even this weirdo can come, but you can't."

HamburgerHalpin: i thought that 2 but i'm pretty sure that escapone was just invited because he can get beer

Smiley_Man3ooo: Escapone does look at least 45.

HamburgerHalpin: srsly. hey--what about dwight carlson? what was he doing down in the basement that day? what do we know about him at all? plus he is weak! fits your calculations!

Smiley_Man3ooo: Oh, didn't I tell you? My mom knows the Carlsons. She said that Dwight is actually Lucille the janitor's grandson. Lucille probably sent him to pick something up.

HamburgerHalpin: why do u keep forgetting to tell me these important things?!

Smiley_Man3ooo: Sorry. I didn't think it mattered. I never really suspected Carlson. If lack of physical strength was the main thing we were going on, we'd have to say it was probably you.

HamburgerHalpin: or you!

Smiley_Man3ooo: I'm wiry!

HamburgerHalpin: u r a noodle

Smiley_Man3ooo: Speaking of the so-called weaker sex (you), who is to say that girls can't be killers? I have looked into the eyes of Purple Phimmul and seen a stone-hearted assassin waiting to happen.

HamburgerHalpin: she might not be that bad . . .

Smiley_Man3ooo: Why are you defending Purple? Are you in love with her?

HamburgerHalpin: what? no. just . . . there might be more going on there than first meets the eye

Smiley_Man3ooo: You totally love her. I, on the other hand, remain coolly detached. We're on a murder investigation. Everyone is a suspect.

HamburgerHalpin: even purple?

Smiley_Man3ooo: She would do anything for Leigha.

HamburgerHalpin: murder? i'm dubious frank

Smiley_Man3ooo: What about Marie Stepcoat? Or Gabby Myers or Teresa Lockhart or somebody? We haven't talked about them in a while. And Kevin Planders clearly has the makings of a homicidal stalker!

HamburgerHalpin: does he when you get right down to it?

I am not paying attention to the clock and am glad Devon sends me a message saying the bell has rung. We walk down the hall to math, sending a few more secret messages about potential suspects as we wind through the masses. Then he sends a little message saying "Look to your right" just as a cute senior bends over at her locker. Nice.

CHAPTER FORTY-THREE

Math class. It is sort of impossible to believe that instead of standing there "teaching" us about angles, Miss Prefontaine is at this very moment in a jail cell. It is hard to imagine her feeling scared, and weirder still because only Devon and I know who really brought her to that point.

Our sub for the day is not Mr. Tough Guy but rather an odd-looking woman that Principal Kroener must've hired as an anti-Prefontaine.

"Hello, my wonderful students," she says after staring at us with a glassy-eyed smile for several confusing minutes. "I am Mrs. Faulk, and you can call me . . . Mrs. Faulk."

What can I say about Mrs. Faulk? A wildebeest in a lime green pants suit. Lipstick smeared on thicker than tar on a country road, and enough rouge to choke a horse. Isn't that what it's called? Rouge? As I try to catch Dev's eye, I catch someone else's.

Hawley, that mustached hulk of a detective, is taking up most of the doorway and looking around the room with a fierce determination. No one else has seen him yet. I alone watch him looming there like a dark troll guarding his bridge. He stares around the room, rakes his chin with giant fingers, and wrinkles his nose as though something smells very bad. And then he finds his man. He is staring right at Devon with a look that could melt steel.

But Devon is just zoning out. I note that he is doodling some dolphins, for nostalgia's sake. Hawley coughs, and Devon looks over at him. He motions with two fingers on his left hand that Devon should come with him. Devon looks at me and does that move where you pull your collar in mock fear—trying to make a joke of it. But as he passes by, his face goes a few shades paler.

Faulk blathers and everyone whispers, speculating on Devon and the detective. What to do, what to do? Suddenly a fully formed plan, one worthy of the Smileyman himself, comes to mind.

First, I write a note to Mrs. Faulk describing a sudden onset of some unnamed illness that requires an immediate trip to Nurse Weaver. Then I write a second note, which I fold and put into my pocket. I raise my hand and bring the first note to the teacher's desk. Mrs. Faulk reads it and, as expected, seems very concerned. A softie. She gestures that I should hurry along, winking at me the whole time. Does she know what I am really up to? I head straight for the boys' bathroom, take a huge bunch of paper towels, and stuff them into one of the grungy toilets. I keep stuffing paper into the toilet, more and more, like a looter filling a sack. Then I flush.

The water begins to back up. I take out the second note I had written in math class. It says, in a panicked scrawl, "EMERGENCY! THE TOILET IS FLOODING! CALL THE JANITOR!" I run into the classroom across the hall from the bathroom, where a freshman math class is in progress with a teacher whose name I don't know. He looks a little baffled by my sudden presence at his door. He reads the note and immediately goes to the classroom phone to page Lucille. I rub my fingers and make a devious evil genius smile. Then I realize I am still standing in front of the freshman math class.

I run out and head to the back stairwell, which leads to the building's basement. A grumpy-looking Lucille passes me carrying a bucket and a mop. The janitor's office is now empty, and I will have at least a few minutes alone down there. Still, I am nervous. As I stride quickly toward the door, I look over my shoulder every two seconds—maybe more—fearful that someone will see me. I have no idea how I will explain myself if anyone catches me. Am I still new enough at school that I can pretend to be lost? Will they suspect me of starting the toilet volcano? Nah. Maybe being the newcomer-weirdo has some advantages? If everyone underestimates you, you can either sink to their level or take joy in proving them wrong. I'm going for number two.

I am trying to remember what I learned in my one day with

Smiley Security Services. I need to see what Devon is saying to Detective Hawley in Kroener's office.

I head down the stairwell and descend once again into the darkness. The unnerving smell of sweaty socks wafts toward me. I wish the Black Rose could be here. But there is no Frank, no Black Rose. Just Chet. Deaf guy on a solo mission.

Inside the janitor's room, that dank little cave, the T1300 surveillance system is turned on. There on the screen is just what I want to see: Devon and Detective Hawley in the middle of an intense conversation.

I can see Dev pretty well and have an easy time lip-reading what he is saying, but I can't see Hawley. Still, it is pretty obvious how the conversation is going: not well. Devon keeps wiping his forehead with his sleeve. Hawley then presents Devon with a plastic bag. It holds his handkerchief, clearly bagged as evidence.

"Hey, I wondered where that went," Devon says. And then, after a pause, he adds, "That doesn't prove anything." And then he looks annoyed and adds, "That doesn't prove anything either. So what if I was separated from my buddy? So what if I actually hated Pat? And so what if you found my handkerchief in the janitor's office? This is all (*something*) at best. Proves nothing." It is hard to lip-read this last part, since Devon is getting agitated, but I am pretty sure the word I missed was actually "circumstantial." Isn't that what they say on all those cop shows? And then he says something I know they say on those shows all the time: "I want a lawyer."

Apparently, to Detective Hawley this request is as good as

an admission of guilt. He jumps up and grabs Devon. I can't see what is happening now; their backs are to the camera. But I am pretty sure that I see something that looks a lot like the glint of fluorescent light on a pair of handcuffs.

I run up the stairwell. It is easier today, possibly because of the adrenaline, or possibly because I am getting used to running. Devon was right, you get pretty fit playing detective, searching for hidden gold, climbing Skull Mountain, et crapera. I sprint into the hallway and join the students from Prefontaine's—or rather Faulk's—room emerging into the hall in a slow trickle. Other classes are emptying too, a wave of bodies. Then the normally chaotic scene of halls filling with students and teachers suddenly goes orderly and still.

Hawley has Devon in handcuffs.

I look around the halls in a panicky sweep. Some people are saying things like "I knew it!" and "Burn in hell, Smiley!" Some are confused, asking each other, "What is going on?" I feel like I'm going to choke, like a cloud of poison gas had been released into the hallway.

A bunch of people whip out their cell phones and start taking pictures, wanting to capture Devon's perp walk. Dwight Carlson, always out of step with everything, has a regular camera for some reason. His flash lights the hall, briefly throwing strange shadows on the gawking faces.

I try to catch Devon's eye, but his head is down. Even if I had made eye contact, what could I do? How can we talk? His hands are bound tightly behind his back as he shuffles down the hall. I had been starting to put the pieces of the whole thing together, biding my time to make my theory fully gel. I know I have some answers and that I can help, but then this happens: they get the wrong guy.

I push through the crowd. I am not a ghost. I am made of flesh and muscle, and I can be pretty strong when I need to be. I shove people out of the way, step in front of Detective Hawley, and stand my ground. He pauses like he hadn't expected this. And then I do something that no one expects.

I scream.

It has been a while since I've used my vocal cords, but I think they still work pretty well. It sure seems that way. Everyone stops and stares at me, including Devon and Detective Hawley. I sign, just hoping the point will somehow get across, chopping my hands violently. A long, puzzled moment hangs in the hall.

Purple Phimmul steps up, emerging through the crowd. "I know what he's saying," she says. Heads turn away from me and toward her like satellite dishes simultaneously tuning in the same signal.

"That's the sign for 'stop,' " she announces to everyone, her normally bored eyes ablaze. She adds, "You guys. He's saying, 'Stop, you guys.' "

I chop my hand a few more times, then nod to her. "And then," she says, "I think, I think . . . that's the sign for 'wrong.' Either that or 'accident.' It can mean both." I nod. I did intend it to mean both. I make the sign for "innocent." I remember being back at Camp Arrowhead learning this sign. They instructed us to move our hands down as if we had nothing to hide. Though somebody does.

"Innocent?" Purple asks me. "Devon is innocent?"

I nod.

"He says Devon is innocent."

Why is she helping me? Was I wrong about Miss Phimmul all along?

And then she signs to me, while speaking to the crowd, the detectives, Devon, and everybody. "How do you know?"

"Because," I sign, "I know who really did it."

I've had my suspicions for a while. But my theory was clinched the second I saw that flash. That flash went through my eyes, illuminating another flash: the one from Devon's camera when he took his stupid picture of the dark. I saw someone. At the edge of the mine. Next to Pat. Emerging from the wall.

My hands start to sweat and my head starts to spin. My stomach feels like it is filled with a thousand lunches of fried ravioli. I can't let the real killer go free, even though I really don't want to be responsible for what will happen next. I spell out the name with shaking hands.

CHAPTER FORTY-FOUR

The buzz in the hallway is so strong that I swear I can actually feel the vibration of the sound waves bouncing off my skin. There is just an intense energy of shock, confusion, surprise, and utter bewilderment.

Devon is shouting. "We can explain it all! Just let me out of these handcuffs so I can talk to Will." Hawley doesn't want to do this, but Principal Kroener gives the head nod that says, "Do it, buddy." The detective slides a key into the lock and pops the handcuffs. Devon shakes his shoulders and rubs his wrists.

Then he immediately signs, "I trust you." I nod. And then he finger-spells a question: "P-R-O-O-F?"

I nod again. I sort of do have proof. But how can I explain? It will take forever. Hawley paces and gestures wildly, muttering to himself. "Has to be the Smiley kid . . . Returned to the scene of the crime . . . He was picked on by that Pat! He lied about being friends with him! . . . Messed with the surveillance tapes . . . Handkerchief."

The thing is, I can understand Hawley's line of thinking.

Devon and I were separated when the lights went out. And, yeah, Devon made us skip past his interview on the surveillance camera. And he kept several details from me during our "investigation." And I did wonder: Am I being impartial in my investigation? Am I being honest with myself? Meanwhile, Hawley is up in my face, shouting at me.

I gesture to Hawley to back up. He gnashes his teeth, and I reach into my pocket and take out my notebook. He flinches, like I am pulling a weapon. I hand it over.

"It's all in there!" Devon yells. "Will has the proof!"

Hawley flips the notebook open. I read his lips. Everyone is listening in rapt attention. He starts to read. I don't catch all of it, but I am pretty sure he says, "Who the hell is Jimmy Porkrinds?" I grin sheepishly and gesture that he should turn the page. He reads again: "Scuzzy guy loves his fingers?" Everyone is looking at me, and I feel my face get hot. I gesture that he should turn the page again. "I'm not reading this part about Miss Prefontaine's, uh, chest," he says. Why did I spend so much time writing about boobs and Escapone? I gesture as if to say, "Can I have that back?" I take it and start flipping through.

It is embarrassing as hell to have all those things I had written be entered into the police record or whatever, but with Devon's innocence on the line, I have no choice. Hawley looks over my shoulder, checking out my notes about everyone in school. His eyes light up when he reads, "Stay away from

Smiley Guy," but I quickly flip the page again and find the exact page we are looking for.

And there in plain printed English is my map and my theory about who had killed Pat. I had crossed out suspects one by one. Finally, there is only one name left, the name I had signed to Purple in the hallway. Next to that I have a map of the secret passage, a list of Pat's awful behavior to explain motive, and some ideas on ways to collect hard evidence: checking the dog hair on the coal against the perp's pup and for footprints in the passage. We have enough.

I trace the route on the map with my finger. And my notes spell it all out for the detective: "She entered a secret passage a few yards from where he fell. Take the path to the right and you pop out of a door a little farther up the path. She got in on the other side, just before the lights went off, and crawled through. As soon as it went dark, she reached out and smashed him with the coal. Then she crawled around the other side. There are no fingerprints because she had her hands inside a coat with long sleeves. And the hair on the coal should match her dog."

I sign the name again.

Devon knows who I mean. He nods. Purple knows too. And I don't have to present all the evidence right then. Because Purple elbows the person standing next to her and translates this in a whisper. At least that's what I assume happened, because the person next to Purple suddenly turns as white as a ghost. She literally starts shaking in her shoes and then tries to flee. Before she makes it more than a few steps down the hall, however, she smacks right into Principal Kroener. The true cul-prit is apprehended.

Principal Kroener is holding her by the shirt. Suddenly the word "collared," as in "The police collared the suspect," makes sense. He just grabs her by the collar and doesn't let her go. Detective Hawley is pacing and huffing like an angry lion at the zoo. He gives her a look that says, "You're not going anywhere, Ms. Pennington."

Leigha collapses; she looks so young, like a girl. A baby. I don't see exactly what she is saying, but I don't need to.

So I'm back at my computer playing around online. Yeah, I solved a crime of national importance, got a bunch of Republicans cleared of assassinating a high school quarterback, got the homecoming queen arrested—just normal-dude stuff. Just a regular long weekend in public school. Uh . . . to be honest, it has been pretty amazing. For the day or two after Leigha's arrest, I was on the local news as the lead story.

I got top billing even before the twin scandals of sexy Miss Prefontaine and the drug-dealing Jimmy Porkrinds, which still have the town in a fury. My name was even briefly on CNN.com. They wrote, "Pennsylvania deaf high school student Will Halbin solves murder of son of casino scandal kingpin Pat Chambers; Chambers cleared in corruption scandal." Yep, they spelled my name wrong. And, yep, Pat Chambers Sr. got off scot-free.

Maybe people cut him some slack because his son died. Maybe he just had a really good lawyer. I still think he might be a raging scuzzbag, but my feelings on the subject changed somewhat when he presented me with a large check for catching his son's killer. All the money that was going to go to Pat's party came in one fat personal check to one William Halpin. Pat Senior said I could do whatever I want with it. I have several things in mind.

Oh, and I even got mentioned on TheTruthIsNot.com! It was posted by someone other than me, I swear. They thought *I* was a CIA hit man, which was definitely sort of awesome.

I spend a while online reading my own press until I get tired of it. But I have one more page to visit. I click back to my old favorite: Leigha's profile page. I'm a weak man. Even after everything, I want to see that picture one last time. I am not prepared for the flood of comments damning and defending Leigha. It is fascinating reading. Some are on her side, maintaining that Pat was an overcontrolling maniac who got what he deserved. The way he treated her was terrible, and she just snapped. It wasn't premeditated or anything. Still, they are talking about life in prison.

Some people just wrote, "We'll never 4get u!" which seems a little inane and obvious. Most of the messages are condemning or downright threatening, including statements like "i hope someone gets u baaaack." Others contain a bunch of words I probably shouldn't repeat (left by people like Travis Bickerstokes, who was understandably shaken up).

From several of the messages, it becomes clear that we had

correctly lip-read the question that made Leigha cry in the interrogation. She was (is?) pregnant with Pat's baby, and he was trying to force her to—how do I put this?—get rid of it. He even got physical with her a few times over it, which explains her increased amount of makeup and puffy lips. This part makes me sick. Pat was worse than anyone thought.

There is one interesting heartfelt message, left by Purple Phimmul, of all people. She simply wrote, "So sad." Those two words really do seem to sum it all up. Pat crossed the line in how he treated Leigha, and she way crossed the line in how she fought back. It is just so sad. I sit there, thinking deep thoughts. I check out Purple's page, catching up on what Purp is up to.

She has some new pictures, including a few in her family's oak-paneled study. There she is, doing her weird Purple face in front of a giant oil painting in the study. They are the type of family that has oils of all the old Phimmuls. One of them—with his giant mustache and super-old-timey hearing aid—looks sort of . . . familiar. In fact, he looks *extremely* familiar. Is it because I read about him on the mansion's Web site? Or is it because he looks exactly like the picture sitting on my desk at that very moment? Purple's caption says, "Me and my great-uncle Andy, LOL."

I stare at the painting of Andy Phimmul and compare it to the photo of Dummy Halpin. Maybe it's the double *m* that gives me a hint? Andy Phimmul, Dummy Halpin! I grab a pencil and scratch it out. A perfect anagram. Andy Phimmul is Dummy Halpin.

And suddenly it all makes sense; well, some of it does.

Here's what I think happened. Just like I walked out of that fight in the cafetorium with nobody noticing, the original Will Halpin found that being unnoticed can sometimes be a blessing. It can offer a chance to escape. Unlike all the other miners who lived their lives in grime and felt trapped by the walls that fate surrounded them with, locked in with no way out, Dummy used what made him different to make him stronger. His deafness was his key to transformation, his key to a different future. I think he survived that 1901 cave-in by hiding in that secret passage. He knew everyone would assume he was dead, and this gave him a chance to make his life over again. I try to put myself in his shoes. Go back and spend another day clawing coal out of the earth to make some mining company rich or just go . . . where?

Where else? He obviously spent some time in town trying to remain sort of hidden—that could explain all the early "hauntings." But the bright lights of the big city drew him like a moth to a flame. I don't know if he hitchhiked, hopped a train, or walked and swam. But I bet he ended up in New York City. And I bet that he changed his name, met a girl there, and started a family. The Phimmuls.

It all makes sense. How did I miss it? Purple definitely looks like me—some ancient trace of Dummy's lineage flows in both of our veins, like deep coal flowing under the Pennsylvania mountains. And she has deaf relatives whose condition was congenital just like mine, passed down to some lucky ones, skipping others.

A few weeks ago, I would no more have considered walking

to Purple Phimmul's house than I would have planned a trip to the moon. But now it just seems easy. I have a new dog, a new friend; it is time I have a whole family too. I am going to shut the computer off, lace up my sneakers, and walk downtown toward Purple's house—her elegant old family mansion. *My* elegant old family mansion. I will walk past the stump of the DEAF CHILD AREA sign. Are they going to put a new one up? Probably not. I don't really feel like a child anymore. I plan to walk far off the safe and wide sidewalks in my neighborhood and plow right into the traffic of the town's busiest road. I have places to go, people to see. Ace is already at my side, this crazy mutt who thinks I'm the greatest thing on two legs. And before long I'll be the coolest thing on four wheels. That's right: I'm taking driver's ed next semester. Hiring an interpreter for CHS and the deaf school outta my own hefty pockets. You're welcome.

Oh, and I'm going to get really skinny and buff. All slim like a swimsuit model. Ha-ha, totally kidding. I'm just like my dad and grandfather and great-granduncle Dummy Halpin. Some people simply like to eat. Get over it, world.

But before I do all this, there is one more thing I have to do.

Of course, Devon is logged on.

HamburgerHalpin: howdy frank

Smiley_Man3ooo: Just thinking about ya, Chet! It's been crazy, huh? I can't believe that everything turned out exactly like a Hardy Boys book.

HamburgerHalpin: except for the part where the quarterback had a sex liaison with one of his educationalists

Smiley_Man3ooo: Oh yeah.

HamburgerHalpin: and then the prom queen got knocked up and pushed him down a coal shaft

Smiley_Man3ooo: Well there is that, but . . .

HamburgerHalpin: and then the police arrested frank

Smiley_Man3ooo: But he was cleared in the end!

HamburgerHalpin: thnx 2 me

Smiley_Man3ooo: I have already thanked you a million times. The Hardys never had such a need for praise. They just solved the case because it was the right thing to do.

HamburgerHalpin: again--i knew there was a reason i always hated those guys

Smiley_Man3ooo: Well, since I need to butter you up, I will thank you again.

HamburgerHalpin: why do u need to butter me up? fat joke?

Smiley_Man3ooo: Quick question--what would you say if I told you I have taken a fancy to a certain ex-girlfriend of yours??

HamburgerHalpin: i would say who the hell says taken a fancy?

Smiley_Man3ooo: What would you say after that? If I said I wanted to ask Ebony out?

HamburgerHalpin: i would say u don't have to ask me. do whatever you want

Smiley_Man3ooo: Great! I hope it won't be awkward if we all go out sometime.

HamburgerHalpin: double date! me and melody

Smiley_Man3ooo: You dog! You asked out that translator?

HamburgerHalpin: not yet but i will

Smiley_Man3ooo: Think she'll say yes?

HamburgerHalpin: dude she has 2. i'm famous

Smiley_Man3ooo: Will Halbin is famous.

HamburgerHalpin: u saw that? haha

Smiley_Man3ooo: Where should we go?

HamburgerHalpin: 2 my party

Smiley_Man3ooo: You're having a party!?

HamburgerHalpin: hell yes--pat's dad gave me a serious chunk of change. i told him i'd rather he make a donation

Smiley_Man3000: A statue of yourself to be placed at CHS?

HamburgerHalpin: a few improvements to the school--a captioning system maybe or an interpreter on staff

Smiley_Man3000: Very charitable of you!

HamburgerHalpin: but i'm spending some of it on dumb stuff too

Smiley_Man3000: ?

HamburgerHalpin: well they already rented that huge place for a party . . . i figured it'd be a shame to let it go to waste.

Smiley_Man3000: 52 invitations?

HamburgerHalpin: why stop there? i'm inviting kids from my old school and a few lucky CHSers

Smiley_Man3000: Whoa!

HamburgerHalpin: still only about 8 at the head table though

Smiley_Man3000: Nice!

HamburgerHalpin: what are you so excited about?

Smiley_Man3000: I just assumed--

HamburgerHalpin: haha. dude of course you're at the head table. it'll be me and melody and you and

ebony and maybe a couple of other cretins. with all
the deaf people there we don't have to pay for a
dj--save money on music and have more cash for
food

Smiley_Man3ooo: Oh, Chet. Still a hungry man.

HamburgerHalpin: and i think i know just what the
centerpiece should be

Smiley_Man3ooo: What's that?

HamburgerHalpin: the deaf child area sign i stole--
i'm gonna jam it right into the center of the head
table

Smiley_Man3ooo: It was you who stole that sign? I
knew it! I just didn't want to say anything.

HamburgerHalpin: u r a true gentleman

Smiley_Man3ooo: And a hell of a detective. Don't
you forget it.

HamburgerHalpin: no way i will my good man

ACKNOWLEDGMENTS

A million thanks to my wife, Kelly, for enduring endless early drafts and never being afraid to tell me which parts were totally lame. This book, like my life, is so much improved for having you in it that it is literally impossible to imagine either existing without you.

Thanks to Ted Malawer for being not only my agent but also a collaborator, a friend, an early reader, and a pro bono psychologist.

Thanks to my editor, Cecile Goyette, for your fantastic, ummm . . . what's the word? Oh yeah: *editing*. (Cecile did not edit this page.) Your humor and wit and style have helped this book tremendously! Will and I feel so lucky to have found you.

Thanks to the copy editors, book designers, and all the fine people at Knopf who worked on the book!

Merci beaucoup à mes amis en France: Philippe Petit-Roulet for the awesome cover art and Manning Krull for making joshberkbooks.com way cooler than its subject deserves.

Thanks to David Galitz, and Cindy from the Beethoven's Ears blog, as well as the deaf writers and bloggers who helped me understand my subject better without even knowing it.

thnx 2 alison nadraws 4 hlp w txting lingo!

And thanks to my writer friends Cyn Balog, Kurtis Scaletta, and all the Tenners for the support, advice, and endless shenanigans!